THE
OF LOVE

By Ron Spates

The Big City of Love
Ron Spates Author

Printed in USA

Published by JM Smith Publishing jks1227@yahoo.com

Contents

THE BIG CITY OF LOVE

This novel is fiction and non-fiction with a realistic turn of events.

The story is about a far distant city unknown to the average person.

There Are Three Ways to Get to The Big City of Love.

First, by Dreaming.

Secondly, by Fantasizing.

Lastly, you're Summoned by the Court of love.

The Big City of Love

The Big City of Love is about the same size of Washington D.C. This City is anywhere and everywhere you are.

The architect of the city is like no other city you have been to. In the middle of the main section of the city you will usually find housing, shopping centers, etc…but in the Big City of Love, instead of what you would normally see in any large city, there is a gigantic hospital like building shaped like a dome.

The dome has hundreds of emergency room like entrances. From each entrance from the outside you will see the lines are as long as miles away.

They are designed to help restore and heal broken hearts. Just like your modern emergency room they are there for emergencies only. This emergency room is not for life threatening wounds but for broken hearts from all around the world. Millions of broken hearts visit the Big City of Love more often than you may think.

In the middle of this giant hospital of healing lies the court of Judgment of love. All of those who have caused great pain or broken hearts will have their day in court here in the Big City of Love.

This is not like a typical court system that has twelve jurors that know nothing about the real you. You are judged by all those who you have caused to have broken hearts and pain. The only way to arrive to the courts is to be summoned to the Big City of Love.

THE BIG CITY OF LOVE "A CITY LIKE NO OTHER"

Broken Hearts are called to the Big City of Love for healing and also to experience happiness, and love, and confidence again.

Being summoned to the Big City of Love is not usually a good thing.

You are summoned when you have broken too many hearts and caused too much pain. You must be judged by the people of the hearts you have broken.

When you enter the Big City of Love you will never look at love the same.

To stay in the Big City of Love you must love and respect others while you're there.

When you enter the Big City of Love you will be encouraged to Live Love and Experience all that is offered at the Big City of Love.

Live: Live the life you have always wanted in the range of fulfilment.

Love: From the very first day of entering the Big City of Love unconditional love will be filtered and experienced throughout your whole journey of love.

Experience: This will be the most unimaginable experience you have ever had. You will be pampered and catered to every moment you are here.

What's so special about this Big City of Love? The Big City of Love has many entrances on the back half of the city walls for emergency healing of broken hearts.

When they are done with the healing process they are then placed in the waiting area where they will be met by their own personal assistant. The assistant will then guide them with what is being offered by the Big City of Love.

The assistant will let them know that everything is five-star hotels, restaurants, etc... it doesn't matter what your true fantasy is, this city has it...this city has the ability to heal any broken heart...that wilfully come through it's doors of hope.

For example they get to drive any car they have ever dreamed of or stay in the presidential suite of the tallest building overlooking the entire City.

They get all this five-star treatment and it only cost love and respect to be there.

While they're at the Big City of Love they get to live, love and experience.

In conclusion, I think that this book will be a great need for many that have not experienced the healing of love, nor the judgment of love.

This will be the most irresistible book you have ever placed your hands on.

It's full of twist and turns, lies, deceit, irony; however, it leads to hope, love, respect, and the power to overcome all obstacles of love and self-confidence, a place where broken hearts are healed and heart breakers are judged. Isn't it time you experienced true love?

A City like no other awaits you and will change the way you see love forever.

CHARACTERS

The Honorable Judge Adam and his twenty-something year old trophy wife, Mrs. Adams. The judge is a very wealthy sixty year old man and is very well respected in his community. He just remarried after being a widow for over ten years. He started dating his secretary and fell deeply in love with her. He promised her the world if she married him. He practically begged on his knees to have her by his side. His current twenty something year old wife is drop-dead gorgeous with a great athletic body shape. To the physical eye she is every man's fantasy and is totally out of control. She cheats, lies, and steals on a regular basis from her own loving husband and this truly hurts this man's soul. He thought on many occasions to divorce her and move on, but he is so in love with her, he can't stand to be without her.

The hopeless romantic, Tracy is a twenty-eight year old single school teacher who is somewhat attractive. She's somewhat shy and gets attached to men very quickly. Her feelings are hurt just as easily. She just cannot keep a man no more than a couple of weeks and cannot seem to find true love. She falls for any man that comes around.

Her day job is a school teacher for the board of education. Her night job is an exotic dancer.

The widow Tammy has three children, and her husband of five years was just killed in car accident. He was the only man she has ever loved. Her whole world was crushed and she cannot re-gain control of her life because of the loss of her first and only love. She was molested as a child and was a prostitute in her teen years. She had never experienced unconditional love until she met her now deceased husband Michael.

The bisexual lover- Star is married with two kids. Her husband of fifteen years has no idea of her bisexual encounters. She's a doctor and her husband Tony is a truck driver. She has fallen in love with a woman Princess and cannot seem to stay away from her. She contemplates leaving her husband and her kids for this woman. Little does she know Tony and Princess have been having an affair for quite some time. They met on an adult dating website. Princess has no desire to leave Tony especially not for another woman.

The sugar daddy Jimmy loves to have fun and still will not hesitate to pay to play. He loves a woman with a big butt and a smile. He will pursue them with lavish gifts and lots of money with that sugar daddy swag to pursue any woman that is willing to play. He's a retired football player who invested his money well. He appears to be tough but he really is a teddy bear. His real motivation is to find true love, but instead he is always being used and abused for his money as well as lavish gifts.

The Player T.J, a thirty year old C list celebrity-famous actor living in the city of Los Angeles always jokes around about settling down to the guys. Instead T.J has a different woman for every night of the week. He has a sarcastic attitude and is a very selfish lover. It's all about what he can get not what he can give in any of his short lived relationships. He lies about how much money he makes, how many movie stars he knows, and how many magazines he's been in to impress the beautiful women he pursues. He uses them for everything possible. One night he meets an ordinary woman that he just falls madly in love with. She ends up using him for his money, his fame, crashes his Bentley and burns his mansion down with him in it. He barely survives the fire and is scarred for life. He can never go back to acting in Hollywood and modelling for the top magazines, or pursue the beautiful women he once had. After that, T.J lost all confidence in himself. He will never be the same.

INTRODUCTION TO THE BIG CITY

Centuries ago before the Big City of Love was developed, the Tree of Life occupied the Land in which it was built upon. The Tree of Life is the foundation of healing and love; and was created to give fulfilment to whomever believed and desired to seek love and guidance. The Tree of Life resided in a far distant land with no known address. It was said to be a sacred, yet magical place.

Well-Funded investors destroyed the Tree of Life unaware of what it was. They were simply clearing the land during the phase of construction.

They developed the land to include luxury apartment buildings, expensive hotels, five-star restaurants and high-end shopping, surrounded by a beautiful city structure. This development was established merely for the elite.

Only the affluent could afford to reside in this hidden gem. The exclusive development was vibrant at the onset but was later abandoned and forgotten.

There were not enough investors interested in setting up residency in the city and the existing residents were unable to sustain its financial burden. They were forced to abandon their multi-million-dollar investments and the city became desolate for centuries.

Even though the tree of life was destroyed and the land surrounding it had been morphed into a development project; the Tree of life was very much still alive but unable to release it's energy to those in need.

Eventually, the roots of the tree started to break through the layers of concrete in the city's foundation throughout the entire city. It reclaimed its land and territory. The entire city was restored and was greater than before.

The restoration was the result of the overwhelming number of people not loving themselves and others. Because they were unable to reach the Tree of Life for it's sole purpose of healing and restoring the broken heart, they began to wander, were confused and severely damaged. They were becoming hopeless and in need of healing - the world was losing love.

The Guardians of the Big City of Love built the city in seven days and seven nights and a full functioning staff was formed for the entire Big City of Love.

The exterior of the dome was like no other city you have ever been to.

In the middle of the main section of the city you will usually find housing, shopping centers, malls, etc...

However, on the back half of the Big City of Love there is an enormous emergency hospital that is shaped like a dome in the core of the city. The emergency hospital has over a hundred entrances. Each entrance has a line forming on the outside that are long as miles away.

The emergency room is designed to help restore and heal broken hearts. Just like your modern-day emergency rooms, they are for emergencies only. However, it is not designed to treat life threatening emergencies, it only offers treatment for broken hearts from all over the world. Millions of broken hearts visit the Big City of Love more often than you think.

In the middle of this giant hospital of healing, lies the Court of Love. This is not like your typical court that has twelve jurors who have no knowledge of you. The Courts of Love is for those who have caused great pain and have broken too many hearts. They will have their day in court and will be judged by all those they hurt.

There are two ways to enter the Big City of Love for healing by fantasizing and dreaming. You enter through the emergency room entrance doors of the Big City of Love.

Once inside, you will go through intake and be evaluated, the ER Nurse will ask you, "why are you here?" and "who are you?" Then you come around to the Big City of Love where you are greeted by the Can-Du your personal concierge and the Guardian Mike-ee and Zow-ee. They are here to guide and fulfil all of your fantacies and personal experiences while you are at the Big City of Love.

No need to explain your situation they know everything about you and rest assured, you are in good hands.

A GLIMPSE OF TJ

"Listen to me carefully, Natalie," T.J said into the phone plastered to his cheek. "This relationship has run its course. I can do this no more ! We are done." He ended the call before Natalie , even got a chance to speak her piece.

"And that is how it is done, boys," he said to the three men seated on a chocolate couch at TJ's mansion.

T.J was adopted and raised by his single mother. She was well-off and left him with a nice trust fund three years ago when she lost her battle to breast cancer.

T.J has no siblings and did not have his father in his life to teach him how to be a man and how to treat and respect women.

Slow jazz filled the atmosphere, contrasting the construction taking place outside. T.J is expanding his mansion. There is a sexy little bar right down the road and soft light spills from an overhanging lamp.

"That was brutal, T.J," one of them said with disgust.

"It was either her or me, Percy. I already got what I wanted. What use does she have now?"

With a throw of his arms, Percy replied, "I don't know! You tell me. Human interaction. How about a real relationship?. Anything but what you are feeding her right now. TJ its just not cool man"

"News flash: all the women want a piece of this man lol. I practically have to ration myself out to satisfy their needs. You know your problem? You are too petulant. One woman is enough for you; that doesn't work for all of us. Besides, where is the fun in being in a monogamous relationship?"

"I have been with Regina for 4 years now and I have absolutely no regrets I really love that women she's all I need." They both stared at each other for a while, neither wanting to be the first to break contact.

"I still can't believe it took you a year to crack down on this one. You even committed to a full time relationship. Your commitment to ruining lives is commendable."

"It felt longer than that! But it was all worth it in the end. Sam, I kid you not when I say this, the sex was mind-blowing. I had to string her along for a month just for that. I feel bad for letting her go now." He said this as an afterthought.

"Don't tell me you are planning on calling her."

"Only if she would agree to a benefit-only relationship."

"You can't swing that."

"I sure can. I have had her eating from my palm for a while, why would you think this would be hard for me?"

"T.J the slayer!" Sam yelled and rushes at T.J.

"Easy! I am not going to do that because it may become complicated with this one plus, I met this tall, slender goddess…" He blew a kiss to complete his statement.

"Where?" asked the other person in the room.

"Why is Ben speaking up now? I thought he was brain dead."

"Oh! Shut up, Sam. Let T.J speak."

After a short chuckle, T.J answered, "You remember we went to that restaurant on the upper side?"

"Yeah! You were supposed to go dancing after that?"

"Nice! Well, we got to the place and as usual, the receptionist was giving me the come-hither look. I have been meaning to get at her but the timing never seemed right."

"Don't tell me you finally did her yesterday while you were out with Natalie."

T.J gave him a look and Ben averted his gaze.

"Are you crazy? I cannot do something like that. I have a code that needs to be kept. Swinging both at the same place is disrespectful to any woman."

"You have a code of honor, and you respect women?" Percy asked with a raised brow.

"Yes, I do. Why are you surprised?"

"I don't think I am alone in this surprise. You treat them like rags TJ."

"I do not treat them like rags. It's a supply and demand world. They need TLC and I oblige them. You talk as if the need for sex is one-sided."

"I wasn't insinuating that in any way, but you know that half these women want stability and a man to go home to."

"I am not that man."

"Obviously."

"Meaning?"

"You have the smell of a wolf about you."

"Now we are all confused."

"I have nothing else to say to you."

"Good," replied T.J and turned to face the two waiting for his story. "Now, where were we?" – sliding his hands together.

"Restaurant. Receptionist. No, we are not doing her." Sam replied with a wide grin. No one noticed Percy left save for the tell tale door.

"We were not there even 5 minutes when she entered in the arms of a Russian man or one of those iron curtain countries. My incredible woman senses ticked, and I tactfully turned around to see who tripped it off." He makes a slow hour glass motion with both hands and excitement erupts. "She had a red dress with a cut that reached her thighs. I can swear her skin is olive and bronzed. Her perfume swam up my head as they walked past our table with the maître d'. Natalie almost caught on, so I complimented her deep cut dress and that solved everything."

"So, you weren't concerned about stealing from a Russian? What if he belongs to a mob?"

"This isn't the Godfather. This is real life and real consequences."

"And people die in real life. Remember Justin from two blocks over? He had an issue with some Chinamen and things went South. He ended up like a dog in the streets."

" OK now that is an overstretched story. Remember he died from drug overdose."

"That's a bunch of bull! Almost everyone knows he only does drugs recreationally. Sometimes once in six months. They made it look like he died from substance abuse but that wasn't what happened. Now you are walking into the lion's den with hands shoved down your pockets."

T.J's laugh is void of amusement. "Even if that were remotely true. I would only go in, hit and come out running. It would be a one-time thing if I find out they have any ties to any sort of dangerous activity."

"Let's just hope your love for bedding women doesn't exceed your level of common sense. I feel uneasy about this person."

"You sound like my Mother!"

"And Percy," Sam added. At the mention of his name, they all turned to discover his absence.

"When did he leave?" they chorused in unison.

"I am sometimes scared when he does that. He reminds me of that movie where they walk through walls."

"You are so superstitious and gullible. Anyway, what's for lunch?"

"But we are not done with the story. Tell us what happened."

"Ha I don't want to kiss and tell on this one."

"Have you suddenly developed cold feet because he is Russian boss ?"

"Don't be absurd! There isn't any proof that he is her boyfriend, even if he is…" His voice trailed off.

"Just be careful, T.J."

"Yea, yea, Mom. I will be extra careful."

"That's enough trust fund baby!"
Trust fund baby, come on now, I make my own money, but mommy's money allows me to afford the finer things in life… He states, as he caresses his 25 Carat Rolex watch.

"So, lunch?"

"I have a hankering for meat and spice. Let's go over to the new Indian restaurant close to Stacy's."

T.J grabbed the car keys from a low table in the middle of the room and turned out the light as they file out into the sunny outdoors.

HOW ABOUT THAT JIMMY

The music is loud and the lights equally so. Naked bodies glide up and down poles with the agility of a cheetah – gyrating slowly and more enchanting. Jimmy's eyes are glued to one in particular and his hunger can be sensed through the smoke-filled room.

The heat rising from his crotch make him slightly uncomfortable and he adjusts to manage the growing bulge. He longed for Peaches so much his body ached. Every part of him wanted to melt into her in a slow deliberate dance of intimacy and vulnerability. He imagined her bouncing ass on the soft part of his thigh as he worked her into states of pleasure.

The only problem was that Peaches hadn't agreed to his advances. She kept posting him to the point where it felt like torture. But today, he was sure he would get into the cookie jar. Everything was set and her response so far had been favorable. Tonight, was Jimmy's lucky night; Peaches agreed to spend the night with him.

…
Spears of sunlight pierce through the otherwise dark room. Jimmy stirred and lazily opens his eyes. As he props himself up on an elbow his eyes

meet Peaches' body. He let it wander, only stopping at places highlighted by the morning sun.

His heart sprang into a thousand melodies and victory tugged at the sides of his mouth. Jimmy's overactive imagination began to replay the previous night and he felt the heat rising.

"Peaches," he called out in a soft voice. The way she slept brought him peace but he wanted to have at her again.

Part of him wanted to make slow love to her in the light of the sun. He had always fantasized about this moment when there was nothing to hide, just bare bodies giving in to each other.

"Peaches," he said again but this time in her ear. He slid out his tongue and played with her earlobe. She felt warm to his tongue and the perfume on her skin barely registered. Her eyes struggled open and a hand flew to shield her from the assault of sunlight.

"Are you awake?" he asked in a tone full of lust.

"What time is it?" she asked. Her voice was froggy; her throat felt dry and painful.

"Midmorning. I'd say about 8 or 9. Haven't had the chance to check the time yet." He stretched his hand toward his phone on the bedside table.

"Yep! Past 9," he declared.

"My throat feels dry, Jimmy."

"Say no more." He was out the door before he finished the sentence. She gulped down the water without taking a breath. The sheet fell to her waist as she sat down, and Jimmy's breath stopped for a second. Deftly, she pulled it back up and tucked the edges underneath her arms.

"That wasn't very nice," he said as he tried to pry the sheet loose.

"Shouldn't you be tired?"

"That is the problem with you young'uns. Old men like me are more virile than the young bucks flaunting up and down the street."

She ran her eyes over his flabby and slightly hairy frame. "Really? I was afraid you were going to throw out your back last night."

"Tell me I didn't do what none of those young boys can do."

She blushed at his statement. Jimmy loved her girly side more than anything. He wished she could become his steady supply of heat, but he knew that wasn't possible.

"What do you say we do two more, eat in, watch television and tangle up like worms in cool soil?"

"But I have to be at work soon."

"How much do they pay you?"

"$10 per hour."

"I would pay for today. Call in sick."

"But…"

"Anything else?"

"Are you sure there wouldn't be any complications?"

"Ask me after the first round is over. I promise you would be too breathless to string words together. Maybe I should make it hard for you to walk back home."

"You are such a dirty old man."

"You are not permitted to call me old man. To you I am Superman. So, are we all good on staying in?"

Peaches nodded.

"Good. Can we undo the protection around those almonds now?"

"Why?"

"I have suddenly become an artist and wish to see them in the orange colored sun." She chuckled at his sarcasm. Jimmy is surprised all over by the firmness of her breasts. The gradual rhythm with which her breathing gave them lift impressed him. He reached out to touch them but got slapped shy of the goal.

"I need food first."

"But this is food."

"Funny. I am famished. Do you want to enjoy today or not?"

"Is that even a question? What would you like for breakfast?"

"Bacon, eggs and coffee."

"I have all that in the kitchen. Let's go." He got off the bed and stops at the door. "Leave the bedsheet there. You don't need it to eat, do you?" She obeyed and stood to her full length. Jimmy beckoned and directed her to exit before he did. He whistled along to the bounce of her behind.

A DAY WITH STAR

"Jason, Allie, get down here right this minute!" Star called from downstairs. The school bus would be here any minute now and her children are yet to have breakfast. Her hair is tied back and held with a clip. Wisps of hair dance in front of her glasses and worry crawl over her face. She takes a deep breath and was about to call out when she gets a peck on the left cheek.

"You have to take it easy, Hon."

"I have duty in about an hour, and I need to rush over to see Sydney before going to the hospital. These children are taking their sweet time and my heart is jumping hoops. How am I supposed to take it easy, Tony?"

"I will handle the children, so don't worry about it. You can go on ahead."

"Are you sure? Don't you have that meeting with Blackstone today? You have been planning this presentation for almost a year now."

"Yes, I have. But isn't it the husband's duty to make the life of the wife easy? Happy wife equals happy life, right?" He moved in close and kissed her full on the mouth.

"Smooth talker. It's a good thing you are not a New Yorker. Don't get too close- your suit will get wrinkled." He pulled her in close and necks her.

Through the muffle, he said, "Wrinkle me some more while I wrinkle your pretty neck."

"Eeew, Dad!" came Jason's disapproval before the sound of their descent. Tony casually looks up and smiles at his children.

"There is nothing to see here. You both should go to school and leave me alone with this girl."

"Mom isn't a girl. She is a woman!"

"She is my girl and our love is a beautiful thing. Nothing new about this." He kissed her on the mouth, then both cheeks then down her neck. Star giggled like a chicken as she pushed him off.

"You should eat before the bus gets here –" The honk cuts her mid-sentence and she shrugged.

"Okay. Hustle. Grab your lunches and head out before you miss the bus again."

"Daddy can drop us off if that happens," quipped Allie who is a replica of her brother Mathew down to the smile and playfulness.

"Daddy has work to do, so we should allow him?"

"I can take them. It's no problem." He wished he hadn't said anything. Star's glare was enough to send him a thousand and one messages, and none coupled with I love you.

"You can't ride with daddy today." She fiddled with her wristwatch and blew hot air. "Look, I am already cutting it close as it is. Can we please get this show on the road? Allie, help your brother."

"Don't forget about the recital on Friday, Mom," Jason said through a mouth full of toast.

"How can I miss my pumpkin's performance. I wouldn't miss it for anything in the world. Now please let's go." Star brushed a kiss on Tony's temple and he waved at them as they headed outside. In the silence of the house, his phone ring was amplified. He looked at the caller ID and a smile split his face.

"I will be there as soon as possible. Breakfast ran a little late and Star just left with the kids. How is it going over there? Orlando in yet?" He paused and listened, nodding a few times.

"Okay. Just stall her till I get there. There are enough copies here to go around. Make sure the media guys have set everything up properly, we don't want a repeat of last time. You know how much we need this deal. Everything may crash around us if this falls through, so please, rally the guys and do any last- minute check you may need to." He listened again.

"It's with Maxwell, Chad & Glover. Call their secretary and tell her I asked for the M207. Becky is a good girl and would help you through the process. Just get it done before Orlando arrives. I don't know how Marge missed this. I told her to get it about two months ago. We are on the cusp of enjoying the fruits of our long labor and all these things are coming up. I would put a call through to the Dallas office immediately we are done here so they can have the joint server fixed.

When did the fault develop?"

Silence.

"Okay. I am sure it is something they can fix in a short time. Uhmm... what else?" He rubbed his temple and shut his eyes. "I will handle everything else on my way out. Keep me in the loop."

Slowly, Tony placed the phone on the table and sighed. It was normal for these things to crop up at the tail end of everything, right? He hoped so. He really did. Orlando would have his head if anything went wrong and with everything going on right now, he can't afford losing his job.

Star was up for a fellowship soon and the children's expenses have been racking up steadily. But that was the least of his problems. He knew the deal will pass if he delivered it exactly as planned. Extensive research always trumped winging it any day and he had done his due diligence. He doubted if there was any speck left in Blackstone that he hadn't seen.
Combing through everything about them had been tedious but it would all be worth it by the end of the day. A promotion should be in order, he thought.

Tony took a stab at the egg on his plate and slowly chewed. He wouldn't rush eating today; that might lead to complications with his digestive system and complications were the last thing he wanted right now. His phone vibrated. He knew who was calling without looking. Today would be a good day, he whispered.

MEET TAMMY

Tammy anxiously looked at her weathered wristwatch for the umpteenth time. The customer in front of her was searching through his pockets for food stamps. Of course, she understood that times were hard and money equally scarce but doing this in front of the line was a waste of time. The snaking line was already oozing murmurings and she braced herself for the request she was about to make.

"Do you mind stepping aside so I can attend to the customers behind you? Of course, I would attend to you immediately you have all the food stamps out." She gave herself a thumbs-up and believed she had been courteous enough to charm a demon.

"Why should I give up my space after waiting all this time?" the middle-aged man said with a cock of his head. His words took her back a few rungs of the calm ladder.

"You are yet to present the stamps and I really need to attend to the people behind."

"Well, they can all wait their turn."

"Sir?"

"Look, don't try to disturb me I am trying to find one more." He pulls out a folded paper and waved a smile to her and everyone behind him. Carefully, he unfolded the paper that had seen laundry soap. Tammy catches sight of a thin female as she walked in and she sighed with relief. She didn't wait for her to finish putting on her uniform before she left the counter.

"Suzzie will handle your checkout, Sir."

"Wait, you are not going to..."

"I'm afraid not. I have to be somewhere."

"I demand to see a member of management."

"That's the office behind those neatly arranged silver cups," She said and pointed in the general direction.

"Hey, Tammy. What a long line you have for me," said Suzzie as she manned the counter.

"I have to go for Chloe's PTA meeting. Thank you for coming in early." She was out the door before Suzzie had the chance to respond.

Outside, the snow stung her in the face and she pulled up the collar of her faux fur coat. The roads will be slippery but she had to make the meeting otherwise the school would start saying things.

It was at times like this that thoughts of Michael tumbled down her mind by the boatload. As she got on the bus, she thought about how life was so much easier when he was alive and how terrible war was.

Whenever news on the Afghan occupation came on TV she felt her heart lunge forward in silent prayer for all those with spouses and family. She still can't stop her mind from replaying footage of the day officers stood in front of her house with news of his death. Five years but the pain was still raw as unripe fruit.

The bus stopped and she realized it was her stop. Quickly, she made her way to the front and alighted. The change in temperature hit her by surprise and her teeth did a musical. Two blocks and one quick stop for coffee later she found herself in the large hall of the St. Georges School.

Parents were milling around a long bench laid with beverage. Out of the corner of her eye, she caught Mrs. Kravitz's wave and made straight for her. Bernie Kravitz was her only friend in the large circle of parents. The woman was wide-armed and transparent. There was no malice in the Aussie.

"I thought you were not going to make it," she said in her usual excited manner. Bernie had undertones of an Australian accent despite moving to the States as a teenager. Like a majority of migrating families, hers came over in search of greener pastures and although life became only a little easier than living on a farm with two pigs and a cock.

America wasn't what they had imagined from all the tales they had heard. But her father, who had a love for hard work immediately went to work and three years later they were among the prestigious families of a little town in the West. She had related her life story to Tammy several times over coffee and chicken soup – both women enjoyed this combo immensely.

"I had to wait for a colleague to swap with. And the line was long and unmoving thanks to a customer with food stamps. Besides, Chloe would kill me if I missed this. I have a lot of X's on her grading sheet already."

Bernie laughed. Tammy found her laugh soothing.

"The kids can be so dramatic. How is the weather anyway?"

"It's draped in white out there. I can't feel my nose. I don't think I have a nose anymore."

"You still do," Bernie said with a wink. "You only look like Rudolph."

"I am always glad to be of help to Santa."

"Where is the sleigh?"

"Safely parked behind Principal Skinner's Volvo."

Both women laugh at the joke. The children had named the principal *Skinner* because of his choice of haircut which for lack of hair looked like pigskin.

"Don't let Principal Groban catch you."

"It is too late for that." Both women turned to face the owner of the voice. Principal Groban was wearing a tweed jacket over chinos with a taut smile.

"Good evening, Principal Groban," Bernie said.

"Thank you for looking over our children so dutifully." Tammy's mouth hung limply.

"Good evening, ladies. If you would excuse me," he said and dipped his head. The women watched him mingle with the crowd before bursting into subdued laughter.

"I think I hurt his feeling," Tammy said with regret.

"Expect a summon to the oval office soon. Don't worry. He would get over it. They all do."

"But that was rude of us – of me."

"You worry yourself about things that are neither here nor there. Look sharp, Skinner is on stage. The meeting is about to start." The lights go off save for the spears of light coming out of the projector that morphed into a picture on the white screen in front of the hall. It was a video of the founding fathers as they laid the first brick that gave birth to St. Georges School. Chloe never tired of this video. Tammy felt glad she could be here to watch it too. They would talk all about it on the way home.

Tammy was seated on the floor of the narrow bathroom that served as her personal space when she needed to get away from the children. They were in the sitting area engrossed in television. Scattered on the pale blue tile were photo albums and pictures of her and Michael. Her hands clamped down on her mouth while tears flowed freely through swollen slits. She had been crying for hours. The memories wouldn't stop playing over and over in her head. Today would have been their anniversary. Yesterday was Dawson's birthday. She imagined life if Michael were here.

The extreme amount of security being in his arms gave her. Michael was the first and only man that showed her what love was; what it could look like if two hearts came bare without any form of hypocrisy.

Men have approached her since his death but the possibility of having anything remotely close to what they shared with him could not be conceived. She figured why waste her time, when all these men could give, was watered down, love. Picking up a picture taken on their wedding day, a smile crawled on her teary face. She remembered the day down to a T.

"Wherever you are Michael please watch over us. The children miss you terribly. They miss you more than I do although they don't know it. I have forgiven you for dying long ago. I know I told you the last time we had a sit-down. I don't know what to do. They need a father figure in their life but I am too scared to even consider anyone. Do you have any suggestions? Martin has been strong and seems to understand the situation I am in but I don't know if I am ready to give my heart out again.

I just wish there was a place where I could get a new heart or at least get this one fixed. I know I need to love again and move on but I don't know how to. If you have any suggestions, I am open."

She closed her eyes and tried to imagine herself in a time when all she had was love. The cool breeze of peace and serenity washed over her face and her hair danced in it. She smelled roses, hibiscus and other flowers she could not name. A swooshing sound went overhead and her heart dipped to her stomach. Tammy's eyes flew open and the scene before her caused her to scream.

She wasn't in her narrow bathroom with smells of piss and cheap detergents. In front of her was a large dome-like building with a ton of entrances. People were trooping in by the numbers. Her knees buckled and the last thing she saw was a tilting sky.

When she came to, she saw herself in a long procession leading to a large dome-like building in the middle. The sky looked pink then blue then a shade of vermillion, but the weather was warm and stroked the skin; it felt like it spoke to the epidermis in a language that encouraged it to grow. A towering electronic board displayed images and a voice followed shortly:

Welcome to the Big City of Love. Where everything is just a thought away. You are encouraged to live, love and experience all that is offered here. There is no room for moderation.

Live the life you have always wanted in the range of fulfillment that have been constructed for your special need.

Love from the very first day of entering the Big City of Love. Unconditional love will be filtered and experienced throughout your whole journey of love. It would be like you have never imagined.

Experience it. This experience will be the most unimaginable you have ever had. You will be pampered and catered to every moment you are here. So why remain hesitant? Make yourself at home. Welcome once again to the Big City of Love.

All the words did were increase Tammy's confusion. How did she get here? Most importantly, why was she here? She hadn't been drinking. Or is this a new technology? But she had no access to whatever this was so how on earth was she here. She turned back to look at the spot that had been empty moments ago. As far as her eyes could see more people were joining the queue. The doors to the dome opens up and a neon green sign flashed Love Emergency. A lady dressed in casual clothing, sensible shoes and a flowing white lab coat walked up to her and offered a smile.

"Where am I?" Tammy demanded.

Without missing a beat, she replied, "The Big City of Love."

Tammy gave her a look that asked is that supposed to mean anything to me?

"I am sorry for my happy nature," the woman said. "I keep forgetting how all this must look strange to you."

"Strange doesn't even begin to cover it. Where is this and how did I get here?"

"Oooh! A straight shooter. How lovely." The woman gave a short, excited clap. "My words wouldn't explain much to you but I can show you around if you would like." She sensed Tammy's hesitation then slapped her forehead.

"What an air-head I have been. My name is… call me Chloe."

"That wasn't suspicious at all," said Tammy.

Nervous laughter from Chloe. "I didn't want to say the name I use here because it would confuse you and wouldn't serve the purpose of gaining your trust."

"So… what do you do here?"

"I am a love specialist. I was assigned to you."

"Whatever do you mean?"

"Well, you have been heartbroken ever since the death of your husband. You have been searching for love and although it is right in front of you, you are not ready to accept it. Long story short? You heart needs a checkup."

"How do you know this much about me?"

"The Big City of Love is responsible for fixing all that is wrong with the world so long as it touches on love. I cannot go into details as to how these details are gotten because I don't completely understand it myself, but I can tell you that you are here because you fantasized about being in love once again. Yes, in the past you have thought about it but your feelings were not as strong as this time. You hit an all-time low in the bathroom, Tammy."

"Don't talk as if you know me! You don't know me."

"Of course, I don't," replied Chloe. "I am sorry if I came off like an authority regarding your life. But the fact is, I am here to help you, but unless you allow me to nothing would change. All I ask is that you follow me and if what I do and show you doesn't sit well then you can opt to leave. I would honestly leave you alone if you decide not to accept my help."

Tammy paused and weighed her words. Everything Chloe had said rang true and although, it felt weird for your life to be narrated by a total stranger, nothing had set off her danger alarm. This woman seemed honest, at least for the time being. Besides, she didn't see any way to leave this place but since this lab coat wearing person had promised to let her go if nothing was to her liking then there wasn't any problem.

"Lead the way."

"You wouldn't regret this," Chloe said excitedly.

They walk into a room filled with machines with tubes running to and from them. There is a wide screen on the wall opposite the door. On the right side were charts and different markings. Tammy looked for instruments that looked harmful or any indication of torture and dissection. She found none.

"Where is this?"

"This," Chloe said spreading her arms, "this is where I work. This is the main channel for handling cases like you. I handle the brokenhearted." She made a hop to a machine shaped like a bed. "This where I run tests on heart temperaments. It helps me gauge how much repair needs to be done."

"So, this thing is supposed to tell you what is wrong with me?"

"Nothing is wrong with you per se. Imagine it this way; love is the nutrient your heart relies on for nourishment but since your husband died you blocked every channel. Of course, you think the love you give out and receive from your children should be enough. And it is that love that has kept you going for so long. The problem is, the heart was fabricated to take in different flavors of love.

Romantic love is one that makes the heart glow with redness. But the receptacle broke when you lost him. All the men that have tried to reach you get a disconnect tone whenever they try because you are unable to receive or reciprocate. I know, you are thinking of your neighbor."

Tammy's surprise was visible.

"How did you know ?"

"It's the city's workings. I just know things."

"Creepy."

"I know!"

"Are you sure this would work? I really wish I could move on and forget all that happened in my past. But every time I try, I feel guilty. Like moving on with my life without him somehow translated as cheating."

"But you know Michael would want you to move on, right?"

"I know! Or rather, I tell myself that he would want me to but somehow I can't get past the thought." She sat on the temperament machine and began to sob.

"I want to find love and be a complete person again but I don't want to forget him. We had so beautiful memories together, you know."

"And living and breathing ones too," Chloe added.

"They remind me of him every single day. It's almost as if they took all of his traits and left mine."

"I understand how you feel. Love is a complicated thing sometimes. Other times we make it so. Moving on and allowing yourself experience love once again wouldn't destroy the memories you and Michael had. Even if you try to forget, the children stand as memorials of him. These are gifts he left behind for days when you need him."

"I hadn't thought of it that way before."

"You are scared of giving yourself to another man. You are scared that he may leave you like Michael did. You know it wasn't his fault but you can't help but blame him sometimes."

"What if I allow myself to love and the person dies like he did? Isn't a legitimate fear? I am not being paranoid. I am just protecting myself. What if?"

"But fears of what if only keeps you from acting and living life to the fullest, Tammy. You of all people should have learned that lesson from years of suppressing who you are. Remember high school when you pretended to be dumb just so you could fit in? The constant looking over the shoulder? It didn't feel nice, did it?"

"No. I hated every minute of it. Then Michael came on a steel horse and stole me away. We went around the country on his bike and it was the best time of my life."

Chloe smiled as she watched her unravel like a flower.

"Are you ready now?"

"Yes."

"Good. Lay back down and think about Michael. Let your mind roam. Dream of your neighbor or whoever you feel you have a future with."

Tammy did as instructed. A translucent screen started from the head of the bed-like machine until it closed off at the foot. Chloe typed on a screen on her wrists and the screen changed colors.

Slowly, a hum filled the room and colored charts started to slide on the screen on the wall. Chloe went over and fiddled with some knobs and watched the screen turn purple. She nodded, smiled and walked over to a cabinet that came out of the wall when she tapped three times. About thirty minutes later, Tammy came out of the machine smiling.

"How do you feel?" Chloe asked with a wide grin.

"I didn't know it was possible to love like that."

"The possibilities ei?"

"Yes! I couldn't have ever conceived that it was possible to give and receive that much. I have always been overly cautious. I just realized I hadn't given my whole when I was with Michael. It feels strange saying it but... how is that possible?"

Chloe shrugged. "Think of it this way; living in the world and going through everything around diminishes your capacity to love. I refer to giving and receiving when I mention capacity. Anyway, even if you had grown up in a loving and supportive family your capacity wouldn't be at a 100 percent. Why? Because the world is broken.

You come to the world broken. What the temperament machine does is return you back to default setting. It takes you back to the way the creator had intended. It shows you the multiple variations you could have taken if you were not so scared of loving. It allows you live out your fantasies and dreams. It does not lie to you."

"It still feels surreal. I feel plasticky."

"It's only natural."

"What next?"

"Well, you would be taken to your hotel room and the rest of therapy would continue."

"What? I thought this was all there was to this."

"You thought wrong. The Big City of Love isn't done with you yet."

THIS IS TRACY

"The use of blank verses by some poets during that century was in a bid to break out of the mold formed by norm. Shakespeare and Frost are still considered greats in the field of writing and their opinions still carry weight to date.

For me, working in strict form or blank isn't the first criteria for weighing the importance or artistic expression encapsulated within. I first try to understand what the writer is trying to convey. The expression is important, so much so that anything that takes away your personality from expression should be avoided like a plague.

For example, Justin prefers singing while Kamau does more of rap and spoken word poetry. It would be wrong to say that one form is better than the other or for us to ask them to compose using the rules guiding the other art forms.

Before these established rules came into being expression was and would still remain the bedrock on which humans create. Bach created so much revolutionary music that he is considered the father of western music. Most scholars studied his music and derived rules of composition from those pieces, yet by some irony, they used those same rules to judge his music. Some failed compositionally while others aced without any argument – don't you find it funny?"

The bell rang and the class was filled with noise.

"Don't forget to do your assignments and poems by Friday. Darryl?"

"Yes, Ms. Tracy."

"Would you like to accompany me to an exhibition on Saturday? Don't worry, I talked to your mother about it and she said it was cool so long as you want to." The boy's face lighted up.

"I would very much like to! Who is the artist?"

"A French man making a debut in the States. I hear his works are good and push the border of conventional surrealism. I know you enjoy Dali's work."

"Is it similar to Dali's?" His raised brow signified the importance of the question.

"Slow down. I haven't seen any of his work but a friend who works at the gallery promises I would be blown. So, this is an invitation to be blown together."

"No Taliban."

"Naah. Hopefully not."

"Thanks once again, Ms. Tracy. You are the best. I would Google everything about him. Give me a name."

She looked at him affectionately. "No. I would rather we both be surprised."

"You know I can check it out on their website right?"

"Yes, but I would rather you did not. I trust you not to." He shrugged and smirked.

"You have a way with men. I promise not to. Gotta go now. Club practice and all that."

"Sure. Get out of here. I will arrange everything with your mother."

Tracy found herself going over the words *you have a way with men*. She knew that to be false. If it were true, Salvador would not have left her after two weeks of steaming excitement. He said she was needy but she didn't understand what that meant.

How is it wrong to give all you have to a man you want to spend the rest of your life with? But it was the same thing with Paul, Khalid, and James.

She keeps falling for men that only take from her. As she packed her study notes, she promised not to fall for anyone that did not show any sign of commitment to her. Tracy knew the will to keep to such a promise was lacking and her heart was as soft as a squid. So, she asked for blindness to hot men and infidels.

Her phone rang and the voice on the other side melted away all her resolve. Rodriguez wanted her company this evening. They both knew what that meant. She felt her head struggling for oxygen while her skin ached to be kissed.

T.J THE MODEL/ACTOR

"Now give me sexy and unperturbed," said the dreadlocked man with a camera. T.J in his boxer shorts obliged and struck a pose. The strobe lights responded to the click on the camera. "Give me 1/24, Anderson." A guy in a flannel shirt walked over to the stand and fiddled with a control.

"Okay, we are doing the last series now. Change the background and give me a Hawaii-esque thing. Throw on that beachwear." After a couple of shots, everything ended and T.J returned in ripped jeans and tight-fitting shirt.

"Can I see the magic we made, Javier?"

"You know I don't like showing these things until I am done editing."

"Yet I always come over and insist until I see them."

"Stop completing my sentence. You are a wonderful model but a shoddy buddy."

"We were never buddies, to begin with." Javier gave him a sly look and they both smiled.

"How is Natalie?"

"Done and dusted!"

"Woah! I thought she would be the one to make you settle down. It was a ruse then?"

"Mum's the word. I would settle down soon I hope but I am not sure that woman has been given birth to yet."

"Pedo alert!"

"Oh! Come on, it's nothing like that. I just like my freedom and all the jobs I have been getting. Settling down sounds good but I haven't found my Jasmine."

"A romantic and a hedonist. What a terrible combination."

"Show me the pictures and forget my choices." He watched Javier connect the camera to a desktop. Moments later, a picture of ripped T.J in *Tommy Hilfiger* shorts covered the large monitor.

"Damn! I look good."

"What is the word for someone that is obsessed with themselves?"

"Self-love?"

"No. The word that sounds like Hitler's people." T.J chuckled. He knew Javier was deliberately making him say it.

"Narcissist."

"Yeah. That one." They watched 300 pictures before T.J was satisfied and stopped the slideshow.

"That was a good job, TJ. I always look forward to working with you because you are just too bad."

"Too bad?"

"It's an expression where bad means you are just too good."

"You Americans and your corny jokes."

"Why are you burning my bridges today?"

"Natalie."

"Dude, I can give you her control if you like."
"What would she do with a behind-the-scenes guy like me when she has had a taste of you? Besides I am happy with Loretta."

T.J rolled his eyes. "What is it with this I am happy crap?" He looked around and whispers. "I need a change of club scene. Suggestions?"

"What is your spec?" asked Javier's assistant Rose.

"Freedom. Zero paparazzi. I just want to be me without any airs."

Rose looked him over and said, "Let me make a quick call to my cousin. He knows all the cool spots in town and is a ladie's man like yourself." The call was over in two minutes.

"There is a club at the edge of town. I will text you the address ASAP." A beep interrupted him.

"Oh. It's here." The exchange is done and T.J excused himself.

"Be careful not to become a slave to your freedom," Javier called out as he and Rose left the shoot. "Crazy bastard."

Six months prior, T.J was summoned to the Court of Love where he was judged by the women who had been hurt by him....

The room filled with a heavy fog of white smoke and T.J fell unconscious to the floor. When he awakened, he was standing in what appeared to be an oversized courtroom with dim lighting and big screen projectors. T.J was unclear of his whereabouts and what was transpiring.

A puzzled T.J stared at the projectors in search of answers. To his surprise, a female by the name of Zo-wee appeared in a spirit form. Zo-wee was a slender woman; she wore a form fitting white dress and had long flowing hair. She introduced herself as a guardian of the Court of Love and began to explain to T.J why his presence was requested. When you break so many hearts you are summoned to the Court of Love, explained Zo-wee. At first, you receive a warning; this manifests into an unsettling feeling in your gut. The feeling persists if the heartbreaker does not amend their ways; hence the reason for your visit today.

T.J turns to face the big screens, with dismay in his eyes, at the sound of the judge's gavel. The lights are brought up in the courtroom and T.J is surrounded by a large crowd of women, 97 to be exact. These were all the women that T.J hurt throughout the years. They were brought here today to pass judgement on him. This was by far one of the largest crowds in the Court of Love history.

TJ's treatment of these women was played out on the big screen. He was mortified at the testimonies. T.J was not a good person. He was known for using women for his own personal gain. He was overly confident, cocky, arrogant and impossible to deal with.

Although, he had been told that he was very selfish and self-centered, he never really thought of himself as that way. He had always thought of himself as a ladie's man; he was very handsome and had a great life – women should be thankful that I give them the time of day (his words).

He was not interested in settling down – just wanted to have a good time, at any cost. His motto was don't get too close, don't get too personal, just have fun! Hearing the pain that these women portrayed in court was disturbing to TJ. He didn't realize that his actions were that flagrant. He had always thought of himself as a good person until today. T.J was very apologetic and pleaded for the opportunity to turn his life around.

T.J was sentenced to 6 months of "no love" – he was to use this time to self-reflect and work on becoming a better man. He committed to changing his path and to learning how to trust and respect women. T.J was extremely grateful for this opportunity.

The courtroom filled with a heavy fog and T.J woke up in his mansion.

At 7:00 pm sharp, T.J was set to go explore the club that had no name. The naming was fitting considering what he wanted to get from there. He was tired of constantly watching his back and acting all civil when he mostly felt like an animal most days. He cast his mind back to college days before the money and the fame. He considered taking an Uber instead of the Bentley. The Bentley won out in the end.

He drove for almost thirty minutes before arriving at his destination. It was a deserted space with no sign of life except for the BOOM! BOOM!! of active speakers and parked cars. Pulling into a free space, T.J parked and slowly got out. He saw a couple and assumed they were here for the same reason as he was. Following them became logical. They went through a bush and came face to face with a hole in a wall.

The surprise made him pause as the couple bent half their lengths and went through the gaping hole. He followed them and met a bouncer at a short distance in front of the entrance.

Entry into the club was a secret code word which made it even more intriguing for his sense of adventure. Strutting like the king of an Island he gave the bouncer the code word and waved him away after being patted down. Inside was like a zoo made for humans. Neon lights, strobes, and heavy bass filled the air like a pregnant cloud. T.J took everything in with the eyes of a skeptic as he walked to the bar.

He ordered a rum and coke and scanned the room for prey. Nothing turned up worth his attention. A group of 6 are playing a game that involved swapping partners and kissing, or so it seemed from where he was.

By his third drink, as if on cue a tall woman walked in and T.J knew she was what he wanted. The air around her swirled with confidence and every step she took was deliberate and unnerving. She sat down three stools away from him but the effect she had on him did not waver the slightest.

He slowly changed location until he is elbow to elbow with her. She smelled of spring flowers and ecstasy.

"I know you can get yourself a drink, but it would be a sin for me not to offer you one." She looked at him like all ladies do when they bid their time.

"Are you the bartender here?"

"No. He," said T.J pointing at the bartender, "serves gin- I am on special duty."

"Club soda and ice," she said.

"Hi, I am T.J. What is your name?"

"Just T.J?"

"Exactly."

"I am Sandra."

"Matches your hair."

"What?"

"Your name matches your hair."

"How so?"

"Sandy with whiffs of brown."

"You are comical at best."

"Come a little closer, I have more jokes to share." He held her gaze for a beat, then she broke contact.

"Are you any good on the dance floor."

"I have learned that magic follows beautiful women."

"You have a way with words. Let us see how well you move on the dance floor."

"It is alright to admit that I excite you, you know." He winked at her.

The music changed into funk and the uproar went up a notch. Both got on the glowing dance floor and started a slow body to body movement. T.J filled his nose with her smell and let the feel of her chest against his control everything else. One song turned into five and five multiplied into seven but the two didn't notice.

They melded one into the other like a special cocktail. To them, nothing existed but each other. His heart beat wildly against his ribcage like a flightless bird while her head rested on his shoulders.

"Get a room!" screamed a group of boys close-by.

"I don't want to wake up without you in my arms," T.J says in a husky tone full of emotion. She looked up at him with eyes that could drown a nation and lips that could heal wounds with a kiss and said, "neither do I want to wake up without you by my side." They fall into an embrace before he leads her out of the club amidst claps and shouts.

"Where are we going," she asked.

"My place." She didn't put up any argument after this but instead followed him in her car. They arrive at the mansion and he lifts her off the ground amidst protests. Their warm mouths found each other in the darkness of the bedroom but T.J pulls back.

"What is wrong?"

"I don't want to rush this. I would like to do things differently this time."

"I don't understand."

"I don't either, but I feel you should sleep in the guest room. I am so sorry. Normally I wouldn't do this. I don't know what has come over me."

"Say no more. Show me where the guest room is." He led her down the hall to a spacious room.

They bid each other goodnight and he walked back to his bedroom cussing himself under his breath. It is not thirty minutes before he hears the sound of his door opening. And before him drenched in the moonlight stood Sandra nude – her body was perfect.

"I don't want to sleep alone," she stammered and jumped onto the bed without waiting for an invitation. "Tonight, is very special T.J, would you not let me make you mine?"

Her forwardness took him back for a moment. "I have been looking for you all my life and the universe has finally sent you to me and I would be a fool to let this slip past."

But something felt off within T.J. Part of him wanted to take this woman from the back until she begged him to stop – but he would not stop.

The other part of him wanted to explore her personality more than her sensitive spots. He felt there was something special about this woman with dishevelled hair. Could this be love at first sight? Nah, it couldn't be. Or can it? All he knew was that he didn't want to go through the same modus operandi he was used to with Sandra.

"I really can't do what you are asking, Sandra. And I am in no way saying that you aren't beautiful. Lord knows I want you right now, but I can't. I have been so reckless with the way I have handled relationships in the past and I really want to change that with you."

"Just one quick one, T.J," she said and pushed her chest on his belly. He held her arms and pushed her away.

"Please understand what I am asking. Please try to understand, Sandra." Her lips searched for his. They met and her tongue muted his protests into muffling sounds. He felt his resolve being replaced by heat and his eyes closed to the sweetness playing on the roof of his tongue.

...

T.J woke up to the chirping of birds and a headache that obstructed his thoughts. The woman on his arm didn't register anything until he thought about it more. The sun came in spears of crimson through the window and washed the room in its glory. He looked at her face closely and wondered how she got into his room. She wasn't beautiful by any means – just a step shy of pretty but her body was a perfect 10. Slowly, in order not to wake her, he pulled out his arm and softly padded his way to the kitchen.

He set up the coffee machine then went out to the driveway to get the newspaper. The outdated Honda Accord sitting in his driveway was an eyesore in the otherwise pristine neighborhood.

He wondered if he had smoked some crack or something the previous night. Why else was this unrefined woman here? That would be the only logical explanation for the woman in his bed. There was absolutely no way he brought back her and this thing back to his house while his full sense was operational. Something was off here, and he was going to find out. He pivoted and stomped back to inside.

Jeffery, his long-standing cook and general housekeeper, was waiting for him at the foot of the stairs.

"Good morning, sir?" said the aged man in the form of a question.

"Very unlikely, Jeff." He swallowed back the rants rearing to let loose out his mouth. "Please prepare breakfast for two."

"Oh?" Jeffery muttered with a slight cock of the head. He was surprised by the way T.J gave the order. Usually, his employer stayed up in bed and rang the bell that summoned him. He rarely ever had enough rump or a *slice of bacon* as he liked to call the female posterior. Something was up today and Jeffery knew better than to ask what it was.

"What would you like, sir?"

"My head needs clearing so coffee. Go heavy on the beans. I would have to ask my guest what she prefers but uh... never mind I leave that to your discretion." Jeffery took a slight bow and smartly headed for the kitchen.

Leaving things to his discretion usually meant T.J had no idea what the person he had brought home liked – a one-night stand scenario was on his boss' hands. Jeffery gagged the laughter that began to seed his face. He was almost done with the eggs and toast when T.J came down. Like a zombie, he drank his coffee and gobbled the toast he didn't want moments ago.

His eyes kept darting towards the stairs and Jeffery wondered what was going on. About ten minutes later, the mysterious guest came down the stairs.

"Good morning," she croaked then proceeded to clear her throat. Jeffery was by her side with an offering of coffee. She thanked him and downed it in one gulp. Both men exchanged glances and T.J shrugged.

"What would you like to have for breakfast," T.J stammered. His eyes were all over her. He felt like a psychologist having a first session with a patient. Only problem was that he was the patient and she was the psychologist – or something like that – if it even made sense. None of it made sense.

What had he seen in this woman? The dress she has on didn't inspire any standing ovation from the organ behind his zipper. There was nothing outstanding about the woman going through his food like a locust during a plague. She was bland. Plain and simple. She smiled at T.J as he served her more food, even the leftover was not spared. "Do you remember much of last night?" she asked with her mouthful. T.J would have been disgusted by this, but surprise took him first. It took a while and her repeating the question twice for him to understand what was being said.

"Nothing much. Just bits and pieces."

"I think I have perfect recall." This was a surprise.

"Oh," was all he managed to say.

If she was disappointed by his reaction it didn't show. "I think we may be the envy of everyone at the club." T.J remained quiet.

"At least, you remember that much?"

"I am truly sorry. It's not usually like this for me."

"Was that your first time being there?"

"Funny. Yes."

"Little wonder! The alcohol there takes getting used to. It's a different mix from what I have sampled around the city."

He raised a curious brow. "You go bar hopping?"

"Sometimes!" she said with a giggle. "Don't give me that look. I like knowing where the cool places are around town. I pride myself to be a map of sorts, besides a girl is allowed to be adventurous, right?"

"Sure, of course! About last night… did we?" He noticed her cheeks turn red.

"No. I tried but you refused." I wonder why, he thought.

"Was it something I did?"

"No!" he said with an outstretched arm. "I am sure you were wonderful company. It is just a phase I am going through."

"It's okay if you don't want to talk about it. It's not like I wanted you inside me that badly anyway." Her words bred an awkwardness that would have gone down in history books.

"What do you do?" he asked in the hope of restoring the air of openness.

"It depends what time of the day you are asking."

"What does that mean?"

"On some days, I am an activist and PR consultant for an NGO out in Ghana and the Islands in my spare time. We produce awareness campaigns and merch to support the fights going on in other regions. My full-time gig is an attendant at a local hospital. And then I make movies with friends sometimes."

"That is an interesting cocktail."

"Trust me, that was the short hand version."

"You do more than those?"

"About three more. I have had to experiment with the things I liked and then work around a schedule to help me keep up. It hasn't been easy."

"We must look like mortals to you demi-gods!"
Her laugh is guttural yet soothing. T.J is surprised by the respect growing in his heart for this multi-career woman.

"It doesn't work that way. I'm what they call a multipotentialite. I know, the word is a mouthful. It only came into recent use, some prefer to be called scanners, polymaths or the jack-of-all-trades. I don't like the jack-of-blah, it just seems condescending. It's just me, I guess. Anyway, did you know that Leonardo da Vinci had about 8 occupations while he was alive?"

"Did you read that from a website?"

"Actually, I did!" she said with a wink. "I had to read up on everything when I discovered my peculiarity had a name and a large community to boot. You would be amazed by the number of people that are demi-gods. My mind was blown when I got to read the stories and meet some of these people."

"I don't completely understand it."

"Well, it is simple. Multipotentialities, the word not the noun is an amalgamation of multi and potential. It means multiple potentials. Now, as a noun it means a person with different potentials, interests, skill, and all that fluff. It means a person that doesn't have one job. Although, that is a shallow way to look at it because some multi's stay in one job while carrying out their passions. Einstein was a multi and he held down a job while working on his theories at night. He said the lull of office work gave him free time and let his mind conceive enough so he could work on solving problems."

"I never knew all you just said but it actually makes sense. There was this friend of mine that dropped out of college halfway through. We all thought he was crazy or following the billionaire's path. You know all this Steve Jobs, Mr. Gates and Zucker story about school not being the ultimate. Blah blah blah." She nodded and stabbed at a piece of vegetable with her fork.

"Anyways, he did the same thing at four more colleges! It wasn't until the fifth that he graduated. I never understood why someone would do something like that when they exhibited no visible sign of starting a company or interest in billions. He used to speak about schooling not interfering with his education, I guess none of us understood the philosophy he was peddling. Guess what? He heads a multibillion-dollar corporation at the moment."

T.J shakes his head and let out a small laugh.

"Who would have thought? I was surprised when I saw his picture in the newspaper."

"Wow! Six colleges before he stuck with the program. Doesn't everyone believe or at least have at the back of their mind somewhere that the third time is the charm?" They both laughed at this. T.J found himself enjoying her company and sense of humor. It was like a sensual dance he had no idea was happening.

"Hi, my name is T.J," he said as he stretched his long arm across the table. The chair he was on protested at being pushed back spontaneously.

"I remember!" she exclaimed but grabbed his palm before embarrassment flooded him.

"My name is Sandra." They held each other's gaze for a while and T.J saw himself actually liking this woman with different careers. As she sat down, Sandra beamed a smile and said, "Enough about me. What do you do? Have you seen the size of this house ?" Her words were cut off and her eyes went wide with wonder. "Don't tell me you are the friend you just spoke about! Oh my God! I have made such a fool of myself blabbing about what I understand only a smidge."

By now T.J had caught on as to why she had stopped midsentence. His laughter rolled through as the house and tears came to his eyes.

"You are grossly mistaken. There *is* a friend that did all that. And you didn't make a fool out of yourself. I would have to know more than you to even think that. I don't."

She placed well-manicured fingers on her chest and let out a sigh of relief. T.J noticed the rhythmic rise and fall of her chest. A flash of remembrance strikes him; those breasts had been thrust at him hours ago but he had turned them down. The chemicals coursing through his veins at the moment didn't mind – they urged him to do more than stare. He drowned the urge in a sea of resistance.

"What do you do then? This house is so huge. And beautiful."

"I am an actor," he replied in a tone only those who knew well the power of the beauty bestowed on them by nature.

"You must be really good and famous if you have this building all to yourself." He assumed she was pretending not to recognize who he was, so he bids his time and waited for when she dropped the act and turned into a googly-eyed fan. She didn't.

"You don't recognize me?" He struck one of his famous poses but no dice. He tried another. She stared at him like a disinterested zoo animal.

"Sorry. Nothing comes to mind." He hurriedly got out of the chair and returned with a DVD collection.

"Look through those," he said and threw one case after another in front of her. She stared at the pictures and placed it beside him.

"You guys look similar, are you sure this isn't your brother?" His laugh comes in cracks. Everyone recognized T.J. He had never had to go through this much trouble before in order to prove who he was.

"Under what rock do you stay?"

"Ha! I am not really into movies and I suck at remembering faces unless they are attached to events in my life."

She shrugged. "I know. I know. It is weird. I make films sometimes so I should at least watch movies, right?" T.J is too taken aback to respond.

"I enjoy making movies but I don't particularly like movies. It is a strange dynamic but it is how I have been for as long as I can remember. I am sorry if I offended you."

The narcissist within him wanted to throw her out of the house but the growing *good man* wanted to enjoy this new experience. He was committed to changing his life.

"It is fine, I guess. I honestly never considered that anybody alive would not know me. It is a good thing that my pride just got a check."

"Do you enjoy making movies?"

"You don't have to try to make me feel better."

"I am not!" she said in a loud whisper. "It is my fault for not remembering but I genuinely want to know if you enjoyed it. I am not trying to make you feel better. Of course, I'm attempting to squelch this awkward cloud between us but it isn't for the reason you think."

Her candor affected him. How can a human be this open without malice? The industry had taught him to be cold, calculating and merciless. This woman's innocence affected him to the point of twitching.

"Of course, I enjoy making movies! I get to see different people, travel, meet girls and – wait, so last night, you didn't know who I was?"

She placed one hand on her chest and raised the other about shoulder high. "Honest to God, I didn't."

"So, you didn't follow me home because of my status or anything like that." He didn't realize he had said that out loud.

"Was that what you really thought?"

"Yes. I mean, No. Look, I'm sorry but it's still unsettling to find someone that doesn't know me and still follow me home."

"So, the natural thought is that every girl follows you for your money and fame."

"Yes."

"Maybe I just like you. Maybe your pickup game was strong?"

"Of course, it is but you know..." His voice trailed off and his fingers ran through slightly damp hair.

"Look, I wouldn't pretend to understand where you are coming from," she said. "But let me take an outsider's stab at how your industry works; everything is plastic."

"That is an oversimplification, but it is quite close."

"Whoa! You have always related to people from that perspective?"

"Mostly," T.J said as he got up and switched chairs for one close to where she was. "For the most part, you treat everyone as if they want something from you. I haven't come across anyone that doesn't. Everything that runs you is a direct opposite to how things run where I am from."

"I am sorry to hear that. They all sound like horrible people."

His laugh was short and drawn. "What if I told you, that assumption is untrue."

"Whatever do you mean?" Her knitted brows made for a curious study.

"Well, we kind of understand ourselves so everything flows smooth like you would expect a perfect system. Once in a while, a greenhorn shows up but quickly learns the parlance and gets absorbed into the world, but for the most part, everyone is good if you understand how things works and you keep your lane."

"I don't think I would understand all this. But I like you. I really do." Her honesty let loose and an arrow went straight through his cold heart.

T.J felt his temperature rise with a sharpness that left his throat dry. His palm became clammy and the room seemed to shrink by a few dimensions.

"I don't care about your money, status or whatever thing you have learned by being in Hollywood. All I want is you. I want to know you."

There it was again; this shameless declaration of love. He would understand if she had a hidden agenda but so far there seemed to be none. The words caught in his throat like a line hangar on a windy day.

"How can you say those words calmly?"

"Because I mean them. Do you not feel the same?"

"Oh-of course I do, but come on! No one goes about with their heart in their hands. No one presents the one tool capable of protecting them."

"I am not going about offering a sacrifice. I am presenting my heart to *you*. I am giving you the power to hurt me but trusting you not to. Isn't that what love really is at the end of the day?"

"You barely know me."

"When has that mattered?"

"It doesn't?"

"I guess it depends. Love shouldn't be based on a person's attitude or past. It is not a reward you earn for being good. It is a gift. I can understand if you say this is all too strong for you and you want to dial it back. It would hurt me but I am willing to go as slow as you want."

"Nooo! I don't want that." His protest surprised her. "I just wanted you to know a bit about me so you don't make silly assumptions. I am no saint. I have broken hearts and it didn't even make me flinch. So, feeling the things I feel for you is making me afraid."

She said nothing but her smile said it all. T.J knew the only way was to stake it all and put all his eggs in Sandra's basket. He pulled out his cellphone and started typing.

"What are you doing," she asked in her calm but curious manner. God! He could already differentiate her voice. There must have been something in the water.

"I am calling all my *girlfriends,*" he reeled out. "I want to be worthy of what you are giving me. Breaking up with them is a step I must take now. I want what you are offering, Sandra. I want to be able to match you."

If the woman was surprised, it didn't show on her face.

DARRYL AND TRACY ARRIVE AT THE MUSEUM a little past 6 as the clouds were letting down drizzles of surprise.

"It's a good thing I follow the weather channel closely," she said and let loose an umbrella.

Darryl quickly ran under its shade.

"It is also a good thing that I followed your advice and brought along my jacket. At first, I thought you were being paranoid but I kind of thought about it later and it felt wise to obey."

She did not say anything to his mini confession.

There was a throng of people at the entrance and they mingled in and waited for their turn on the line. The man in charge of the list was wearing a penguin suit, he waved at them the moment they came into his line of sight. Tracy and Darryl pushed through until they were at the front.

"Good evening, Richard," she said without missing a beat.

"Good evening, Ms. T. I see you are unnaturally late today."

"Well, things needed doing and no one else was going to."

"Is this young Darryl? My pleasure, sir." Richard extended his gloved hand for a shake and Darryl was taken aback by the courtesy. Finally, he too put his hand forward and the ritual of gentlemen was done.

"We have heard so much about you," Richard continued with subdued excitement. "You are one of her brightest students and we have great expectations of you."

"This looks like a modern-day Dickens setting." Richard's laugh shocked him. It was loud and violent. He tore out tickets, ticked off their names from the list and ushered them into the museum.

"Have a wonderful evening."

THE RELATIONSHIP CONTINUES

The Huang Café offered one of the best choices for breakfast according to T.J and although Sandra argued that she knew a better place everything came down to the moment she bit down on her waffles.

"The raspberry syrup. O, my God! This is so delicious. I never knew food could taste this delicious. I feel my insides transforming into beautiful organs." Bits of food escaped her full mouth as she spoke.

T.J was more amused by her excitement than the destruction of table etiquette. They have been seeing each other exclusively for almost two months now. Life with a genuine girlfriend was all he had expected and more. It wasn't about the sex – although that was great – it was something he could not place his hands on.

Every day, regardless of whatever flaw came up, something within him assured him that he had a goldmine on his hands. It sounded bizarre whenever he tried to explain it to anyone other than the council that convened in his head, so he had given up on trying to. All his friends have teased him, but it didn't matter one bit. He was with a special girl and the world could end right now for all he cared.

"I told you the food here was *the* best." She bobbed her head.

"I am sorry I doubted you." He looked at her neatly combed hair and remembered how dishevelled they were moments ago after their usual roughhousing.

Proving his fidelity to her by cutting ties to anything that wears a skirt and constantly affirming she was the only thing he wanted, was a double-edged sword he still didn't understand.

It still boggled his mind that until their meeting she had no idea who he was. He was irritated and thought she was being pretentious about it that morning, but gradually, her sincerity had won out.

T.J found his compatibility with Sandra strange but right. They both belonged to different sides of the system, but she seemed content enough with her salary as an attendant at the local hospital; she had changed three jobs since they had met. He liked the fluidity of her decisions, but it was the way she talked that made him realize how much he loved her – yes, he did, without any hesitation. Admitting that much to himself did away with the shame that was building up within his chest especially after she ate her share of food and his that morning. Who does that on the first sleepover?

"What are you doing after here," he asked.

"Nails, face then the hospital. I have duty today and no, it can't be put off." T. J's disappointment was abundantly obvious, but she ignored.

"Why are you acting strangely. You know I have to be at work. I have been putting off and asking Regina to fill in for me, don't you think that at some point she would become tired and touchy."

"At some point, yes, but not today."

"You are being selfish again."

He raised his hand to signal withdrawal.

"I apologize. It's just that I want more time with you. The more I spend, the more I want to. Please try to understand this. Besides, it's not like you need the money. I have enough to keep us both high up in the sky."

"Baby, you don't expect me to give up my work and leech off you, do you?"

"I do! Please, Leech off me." T.J says sarcastically.

"You are deliberately being difficult. You know it isn't really about the money for me. What would I do with my time if I take this offer? How am I supposed to find fulfilment?"

"Easy," he said with a shrug of his shoulders.

"Isn't it satisfying to be satisfying me?"

"Be serious please!"

"Look, I was only joking around but please think about it. I really love you, Sandra. There is no one else for me but you. Whenever I get like this please understand that I am just expressing my true feelings. I am surprised by my own need for you."

"Natalie called your phone yesterday."

"So?"

"I thought you said everything was over between you two."

"It is. But I have to meet her sometimes because of work plus I am not in-charge of her phone."

"No one likes a smarty pant."

"I do. I have told you that I have nothing to do with anyone else. Those bridges are long gone. It will always be you unless you choose to – I can't bring myself to even think it so let us forget I said anything."

"Unless I choose to what? Leave you? Is that how much you think of me?"

"No. But you always doubt me. Like the last time, you showed up at my meeting because you assumed, I was lying."

"I apologized about that. I didn't know what came over me. I am really sorry."

T.J wondered if the sorry would translate into not repeating the same action. Sandra had broken into his meetings several times, it was getting hard to manage. The woman just wouldn't bring herself to trust him.

"I hope this is the last time something comes over you and pushes you to come breakup a good deal."

"Are you giving me an ultimatum? Is this what this is? You brought me out here to butter me up and show me what I would be missing if I left you? Go on, say I am lying."

"This is ridiculous! Your intrusions are making work hard for me. People are afraid of working with me. I am only telling you because it affects us both. I am not giving you an ultimatum, although now, I wish I were. Stop barging into those meetings. If I say I have an appointment, just believe me and let things go. Please." After all, I am running a business.

"Is it wrong for a woman to check up on her man?"

"It is when she suspects him of cheating or breaks into a meeting that had been carefully planned. I lost three endorsements this month." It was almost as if she was a demon sent to torment me and destroy all that I have worked hard for. (He did not say that part out loud). It stayed in his realm of thought.

"I am sorry, baby. I will try. Sandra is a good girl. Sandra will try." She reached out and kissed his forehead. Then his mouth.

He signalled the waiter, settled the bill and left. None of them would be going to work today. Maybe later. Much, much later.

Exhausted from their labor, two bodies break up. Each taking in gulps of air and trying hard to level breathing. They looked at each other and one is flooded with pink cheeks.

"I was unsure of coming here today, but I must say…"

"Don't say anything, Star. You were incredible. Where have you been hiding that body?"

"In my husband's house."

"We need to get over to mine more often, don't you agree?"

"Absolutely. It was almost like you knew every part of me."

"Did I not promise to be the best lover you have ever had?"

True she had made that promise. It was also true that Star had fallen hopelessly in love with her even before the exchange that just happened. For a while, she had felt like her sexuality went both ways and Princess was responsible for egging her on to experiment.

This beautiful exhausted woman that knew exactly what to do to turn her on had told her it was nothing to be ashamed of. What would her husband think? Their children? Was she going through a midlife crisis?

"What are you thinking about, my love?"

"My family."

"I am right here and you are already thinking of your husband? I am truly hurt."

"No, it's not like that. You have my heart, you know that right?"

"Then what are you thinking about?"

"How all this is surreal and you know." She turned on her side facing Princess. "What will my children think of me? What will happen to my career?"

"But no one needs to know."

Star frowned and chewed her lip. "You want me to keep this a secret? Do you not love me?"

"Don't say absurd things, darling. You very well know that I do. I love you. It's because of the love I have for you that I don't want to see you go through the hassle of public scrutiny."

"But it wouldn't be fair to my husband."

"Star, I love you but can you ease up on the *my husband* talk? Call his name or something else."

"You are cute when you get jealous. Keeping this wouldn't be fair to Tony. There I said it."

"Look, if you feel outing us would make you feel better then fine. But really, what will it get you? We see each other whenever we want to. For me, being happy is staying here with you. And announcing our love to the world wouldn't change anything."

"It would save us the energy of sneaking around."

"Which is romantic in its own right," quipped Princess.

"You just want me to yourself, don't you?"

"How did you figure out my well-guarded secret? This booty belongs to me."

"Yes, it does."

"Come here let me look under the hood. There are some tunings to do before you are free."

THE FIRE

"What do you mean it was nothing? She was on your lap playing with your beard." The veins were visible on Sandra's forehead and T.J was at a loss on how to handle the situation. T.J was really trying to be a good person, but he kept going down the same path. He could not resist the desire and urge for other women, and Sandra was privy to this.

"Look, it was a shoot. These things happen. I know it looked like you caught me in a compromising position, but it really wasn't the case. Why would I get something on with her in front of everyone?"

"Oh! If you were alone things would have been different, is that it?"

"You are being unreasonable."

"Don't tell me what I am being. I know what I saw. She was flirting with you and you were encouraging her. You talk about all the people there." She hissed and paced the floor. "Is it not common knowledge that people in Hollywood are unfaithful? It is encoded into your genes!"

"Can you stop and listen to yourself speak for a second? Until a while ago you didn't even know me or the fact that I worked in *that* industry. Now, you are suddenly an expert on all things Hollywood? Come on!"

"It doesn't matter how you choose to twist this thing. The fact is you can get it on anywhere you want, and you were certainly getting it on with her. What's her name anyway?"

"Ciara."

"I feel bad for clawing at her without knowing her name or introducing myself. But you know it was all for you right, baby?"

"That wasn't for me, Sandra. I keep telling you that I have nothing to do with those girls – it's all about you baby. That was a shoot for a new drink that is about to hit the market. You have ruined the face of a new rising model that is growing in status. What if they sue? Do you not understand the ramifications of what you have done?"

"She can sue?"

"Like hell, she can! I had to put Jack on it immediately. I hate calling my lawyer dude about things like these. We had agreed to keep my shenanigans to a minimum. But your string of abuse will put me back up in the eye of the press. You keep undoing me, Sandra. What have I ever done wrong other than love you?"

"I am sorry. I only came by to wish you luck. Something within me just let loose when I saw you like that. I know I keep saying sorry, but I really mean it."

T.J put his head in his hands. "You believe me, right?"

"I don't have the strength to deal with this right now. Can we please just go to bed? There is no need to stress over things this night." Sandra attempted to continue the conversation as she followed T.J upstairs to the bedroom -but T.J shunned her away.

Sandra snuck downstairs to the bar after T.J fell asleep and drowned her sorrows in Jack Daniels. After downing a bottle, she stumbled up the stairs into the bedroom to continue her conversation with T.J. She stood over his limp body as he slept and mumbled – "You are going to pay for this."

Sandra made her way down the stairs and into the garage with rage in her eyes. The vengeance in her heart gave her the momentum to make her way to the gas station to fill the 10 gas cans that she had placed in the trunk of TJs car. When she made her way back to TJs mansion, she went into the safe, (T.J had entrusted her with the passcode) and filled a large duffle bag with $5M.

Sandra packed T.Js car with her clothing, personal items and the $5M in cash and headed back into the house. She grabbed the gas cans and began to pour the gas throughout TJs mansion. After she filled the house with gas, she set it on fire. Sandra ran out of the house before the flames erupted, driving off in TJs Bentley with jealousy and envy in her heart. As she drove away, she muttered, "You will never cheat on me or anyone else again T.J."

The fire alarm snatched the sleep away from his eyes and T.J jumped to life. There was smoke everywhere, he could hardly see. This all felt like a night mare, but T.J was very much awake. The heat and smoke stung his eyes and he coughed a few times. He half expected his insides to spread on the floor.

"San – Sandra," he called out as he felt the bed for her with his left hand. There was no sign of her. The bout of coughs came once again but this time he vomited the contents of his stomach onto the bed. The smoke overwhelmed him, filled his lungs and T.J eventually passed out. Outside, the siren of the fire department approached the mansion. They found their way into the mansion and was able to uncover T.J's body. The enchanting mansion that was once the envy of the town slowly crumbled under ember oppression.

The drone of the hospital AC brought him back to consciousness. Tubes are flowing from him to machines gathered around his bed. Forcing one eye open, T.J tried to sit up but the searing pain running throughout his body and his face drew a scream from his aching throat. The door opened and a nurse came in with a clipboard. She runs back out and returned momentarily with the doctor.

He could see their mouth move but couldn't make heads of what was being said. Slowly, he began to tune in and understand what the doctor was asking.

"Where am I?" and "What happened to me?"

"On a scale of 1-10 how would you describe your pain?"

"A 20. Can somebody explain what the hell happened to me?" "Why am I here?" "Was there an accident?"

"It will come to you in bits and pieces. You hit your head pretty bad when you fell from the bed."

"Bed?" His memory flashed and he remembered smoke and fire. "Where is Sandra? Is she alright?"

"She is," replied the nurse as she gave the doctor a look that bode secrets.

"Why isn't she here? What is happ– " he choked on the last word and the nurse brought a cup of water to his lips. He drank it hungrily before collapsing back on the bed.

"Poor guy," said the doctor. "I don't want to be the one to break the news to him. Such a shame."

"And to think he was such a wonderful actor. Why do bad things happen to good people?"

"I don't know, Janice, but this is just terrible. Have they still not found her?"

"Nothing. Almost as if she is a ghost. The police put out an APB on her, so we still have our fingers crossed." T.J drifted in and out of consciousness so all he heard were bits of the exchange between the medical practitioners at the foot of his bed.

In his dream, he saw fire and a cloud of smoke, but he saved Sandra and they rode on a white Unicorn with a pink horn. The dream seemed implanted but somehow real. He was concerned by her absence in the hospital but a part of him convinced himself there was nothing to worry about maybe she just went down to the cafeteria because she got famished.

Slowly, a darkness covered him, and a blanket of peace took away the consciousness of his environment. Two days later, T.J regained complete consciousness and the same doctor and nurse were at his bedside.

"Good morning, T.J. Do you remember me?"

"Only a bit. I was out of it the last time from the pain medication. Wait! I need answers. What happened to me? Why am I bandaged up and in agonizing pain? And, what is that stench in here? It smells like burning flesh."

"I am Doctor Morgan and this my assistant Nurse Janice." Morgan flashed a little flashlight over T.J's eyes and asked about his pain.

"My head is throbbing. It feels like Electric music is playing inside of me."

"The medication I am putting you on will solve that within days. I should be back by tomorrow and I expect you will feel a little better."

"I expect to be discharged within days. Let us keep the optimism."

"The police are here to see you," Janice announced.

"Okay, T.J sleep well and don't move a lot. I have told them not to do anything that will get you agitated."

"It's the police, Dr. Martin. Their usual operation is agitation. Where is Sandra anyway? I haven't seen her since I fell ill, and I am worried."

"Not to worry. The police will fill you in on any gaps in your memory."

Two officers walked in and nodded curtly as the doctor and his assistant filed out. He stopped at the door and gave a final warning, "I understand you need to do your job, but don't get him riled up."

"We will try our best," replied the short one. He looked like a doughnut in a uniform and T.J stifled the urge to laugh. He wondered why they were here and how Sandra was connected.

"Did Sandra do anything wrong?" he asked before they took their seats.

"We would ask the questions if you wouldn't mind. My name is detective Henson, and this is Denton." So, the fat and short one was Denton, how apt.

"I do mind. I am grouchy and easily irritable right now."

"We apologize, we would make this as brief as possible and would be out of your face."

Something about the way Henson looked at him when he said face did not sit right with T.J.

"Get it over with then."

"How much do you remember?" It was Denton.

"Not much. The night is still wrapped in fog. I feel like I am wandering in a forest."

"So, you don't remember the accident?"

"I keep wondering."

"What happened on that night then? Can you at least remember? Did you get in a fight or something?"

"With Sandra?" He tilted his head a little to the left and closed his eyes. It shot open almost immediately. "Yes, she came over to the set and disrupted everything. We got back home and talked it over. Oh! My head is hurting and why does it feel like my skin is burning off my body.

"Please take it easy," implored Henson with an eye on the door. "According to an eyewitness report, you both left the shoot a little past 6. Now somewhere between that time and 9 pm a fire was started in your house and Ms. Sandra Liebmann is the prime suspect."

"Get out of here! Why would you think Sandra would do something like this? Wait, fire?"

"Yes. The reason you are in this situation is because of the fire that was started while you were asleep. It would be pointless to ask you if she was there with you during the fire because this isn't the first time she was involved in something of this nature. Although, you are the first to survive."

T.J looked at Henson as if he was speaking Mandarin.

"This is hard for me to say and I apologize if I overstep," he continued, "but the fire was meant to kill you. Your car is missing. The lab guys have analyzed the wreckage and are positive she left with a ton of your possessions. Your fire proof safe was totally empty. Did she have access to your safe?"

Oh God! Yes, she did.

"We are still searching for her and doing our best possible to ensure this gets resolved in time. The doctor says you have to be in here for at least six months. We wish…"

"This is the first I am hearing of this. Six months? What do you mean six months?"

The doctor appeared in the room and the officers bade T.J goodbye.

"What were they talking about, doctor?"

"I want you to listen carefully to what I am about to say, this isn't the end of your life and things will look up after therapy."

"Therapy, What for?"

"You have been covered in bandages all this while and been unable to sit so you may not have noticed but you have 3rd-degree burns on about 70% of your body."

You have been unconscious for 5 days due to the trauma and shock to your body. You arrived unresponsive and were on a respirator for the first 2 days as you were unable to breath on your own.

I have been keeping your wounds clean to prevent infection but now that you are awake you will have to endure multiple showers per day to accelerate the healing process.

I must warn you that the showers are brutal and extremely painful – you will see particles of skin shed from your body as you shower and at first sight might cause nausea and vomiting but know that I will be here with you and will see you through. As your skin begins to heal, the pain and suffering will subside.

T.J kept quiet and let this news sink in. "You barely made it out alive and we were all so relieved when you came through. It breaks my heart to have to tell you this."

"So, I can't act or model anymore? I have a major movie to prepare for. What am I to do! My life is ruined..." He spoke in a slow, absent-minded tone.

Doctor Morgan opened his mouth to speak but thought against it. Quietly, he exited the room after T.J's monotone repetitions. T.J asked his nurse for a mirror so that he could see himself. From what he could see through the bandages, he slowly began to cry and moan as he looked at the new image of himself. Darkness and sadness filled the room.

BACK TO TRACY

It's another Saturday night and Tracy is at the Honolulu club for work. She was one of the exotic dancers and a crowd favorite. In front of the mirror, she adjusted her headgear and the feathers around the slope of her waist.

The room is in disarray with numerous costumes in and out of boxes and a cloth rack over by the end of the wall. The bulbs arranged on the mirror are the only source of light and in its light, she skillfully applied lipstick then rubbed her lips together until it felt right.

At 28, Tracy was an accomplished dancer having studied classical and traditional dancing at a conservatory out in the Queen's land. But she hadn't gotten any professional gigs in a long time so she turned to dancing at strip clubs in order to scratch the itch.

Teaching was the only other occupation that she was good at; she could teach art and beautiful minds. Her love life was in shambles and all the guy's leave soon after they touch down. It was easy for the tentacles of her heart to attach to whoever was close-by and this has been her problem with love. No one needed her like she needed them. They either called her clingy or needy when all she wanted was someone she could pour herself into.

Her recent breakup with Derek had sent her down into the water department. She had held on to hope that he would be the answer to all her cries and for a while, he seemed to be different from the men she had met. But everything changed once she let it slip that she loved him. He acted like it didn't bother him at the time, but she was sure it was the reason behind his lack of interest in the relationship.

It was still hard for her to understand what was wrong with a woman declaring love for a man.

Both genders had a heart built into them, so why does society favor the declaration of one while frowning on the other? And boy, did she love Derek. He was the type her parents would like for an in-law but he just had to be like the *rest* of them. She felt anger and bile rise up from within her, then the tears came down in a fresh torrent, ruining her makeup. Her heart was tethering at the edge and one more push would spell sudden doom for her.

She wished there was somewhere she could go where everything was better and love was a language that was not misunderstood. She longed for a man that would love her beyond her naked body; for one that would reach deep into her soul and cause it to flourish. Would she ever find love in this world of broken standard and systems? A box of Kleenex was close-by and she pulled from it. The knock on the door brought her attention to the present.

"You have five more minutes."

Tracy nodded then blew her nose. Then suddenly it happened. The wall in front of her fell away and in its place was a blinding light. She heard sounds so beautiful that her ears felt liquid. The hair on her skin stood on edge and her heart raced with fear and excitement.

For some reason, she could smell love. She knew it was love. Someone pushed her from behind then she saw that she was part of a long line heading into a large dome. Attached to her right arm was a broken heart symbol with the words *incompatibility*. Everyone else around her and on the queues she could see had the same thing but with different taglines. It was finally her turn and she stepped into the entrance of the large building. A man in blazing light smiled at her and ushered her in.

JIMMY'S TURN

Jimmy and Peaches have been hitting the sack for close to two months now. Sleeping in and having long lasting face-time has become the bedrock on which their superficial relationship is built.

For Peaches, nothing was sweeter than taking Jimmy's money and flaunting in his car. She refuses to do any social function that involved meeting people with him and demanded he did not call her his girlfriend in front of people.

"But it's my friend's birthday. I have told him a lot about you and he is looking forward to meeting you."

"But, daddy bear, you know I don't like going out much unless we are going shopping. Which reminds me, you promised to get me that new handbag."

"Stop changing topics. This is important."

"And getting the bag isn't? I thought you said you were going take care of me if I become your woman."

"Have I not taken care of you? How many places have we visited since you became mine? Answer me."

"You know this bag is important, daddy bear. Don't I also take care of you? Don't you like how I put it in you?" She slowly moved up his legs and set her behind squarely on his crotch. Her hands went down his pants while she moved her waist in a circular pattern.

Jimmy threw back his head and moaned. "You know I won't give up this magic. You are the best thing that has happened to me."

"You sure, daddy," she whispered in his ear then licked the lobe.

"Ah-bsolutely."

"What about the bag?"

"We have to -" she slowed down her movement then shoved her hand deeper. "I will give you the money."

"Promise?"

"Yes."

"Would you like to hit that now, daddy?"

"Let me free, Peaches. I am going to hit it so much you would wonder who this bear is."

"That is right, daddy. Teach me."

...

Peaches left afterward and Jimmy was left alone with his thoughts. He admitted that he was a slave to Peaches and the girl wanted nothing but his money.

The cycle had started after his first wife left him. It was a time when pro football meant everything to him. The victories and trophies had gone into his head and he lost sight of what was important. When unattended, love tended to go away unnoticed and his life is a testament to that truth.

Naomi was a good woman. She had stuck with him from high school until he made the big leagues. He blamed himself for being reeled in by the allure of fast cars and pretty woman.

Although he realized his mistake early on, the mess he had made could not be erased. The woman simply refused to keep up with the string of affairs that he brought back with him. Impregnating two teenage girls was a scandal by its self.

He remembers how unrepentant he had been at the time. He was insensitive to her needs and lashed out at anyone that tried to tell him to act differently. He was a Ronin. A reckless, beast of a man out for only himself. It was around this time that he appeared before a court he knew nothing of.

The court of judgment of love it was called if he remembered things correctly. There he was in his pajamas in the middle of the large court. A haughty Naomi pointing an accusing finger in his direction.

Shortly after that, all the women he had broken by his waywardness appeared and made their case. Jimmy felt naked before all those accusations.

Hearing how his actions had destroyed, devastated and left some of these women stuck in life struck an ugly chord within. The roof of the court had opened and a great being overshadowed him.

"Jimmy, do you know where you are?" the being bellowed.

But strength had left Jimmy. His lips quivered like a leaf in the breeze. He stammered in the negative.

"Your case has been brought before the great council," he continued. "You have been tried and found wanting. How do you plead?"

Suddenly, a man appeared beside Jimmy and declared, "my client is guilty of every charge brought before this honorable court, but I beseech that you be merciful in your judgment.

Everything he did was from naiveté. It's the arrogance of youth, my Lord. Look not upon his great transgression but upon the ability of man to change. It is the ability within man to change and become a creature full of love and the quest for love that is the foundation of every principle in this great Big City of Love."

The attorney then turned to Jimmy and winked. "I know this is all strange to you," he whispered.

"It was the same for me the first time I came here but look at me now, I get to save people from their mistakes and I am happy. Allow me to handle this case if you ever want to live a happy life."

Jimmy was too dazed to reply. A limp nod was all he managed.

"Very well," came the being's reply. "I have heard all you have said and I am of a mind to give him a second chance if he shows that he is truly sorry."

"He is sorry!"

"Can-Du! Let him say it." The attorney bowed low and retreated behind Jimmy.

"Prove to me that you are worth saving," Can-Du said.

Jimmy stood there and scanned the faces of his accusers. He felt an overwhelming surge of sadness and empathy. Seeing what he did caused something within to stir.

He couldn't remember what happened after that but he was sure he had been forgiven because the feeling of dread he had at the beginning was gone after he woke up.

This was two years after the incident and his quest for love was still on. He knew beyond doubts that he would find love – that it existed and was tailor-made for him. Peaches may not be the one for him but he would treat her like the goddess that she was and hope that someone else was treating his love with great respect.

The doorbell rang and he hurried to the door. In tears and tattered clothes stood Peaches. She flew into his arms the moment he opened the door. Jimmy pulled her tight without asking questions, those would come later. Right now, this woman's soul needed to be protected and only he could do that, he thought. She laid her head on his lap until she calmed down. The tears were still coming but the shivers had stopped.

THIS IS STAR

Tony put out the *do not disturb sign* and slowly closed the door behind him. Lying on the bed with nothing on was Princess. The woman looked beautiful without any effort. He always thought beauty made her home in Princess.

Since their physical meeting two months ago, everything has been on the up and up. She was his soul-mate in more ways than one. It wasn't about the sex for him – he felt a real connection with Princess. Her simplicity ensnared him and kept him grounded whenever he wanted to go off on a trajectory.

"Well don't just stand there. Dig in," she said in her usual seductress tone. It drove him absolutely nuts when she spoke to him that way. He felt like devouring, exploring and carefully saving parts of her every time she invited him to eat her delightful body.

He unbuckled his pants and flung them with the kick of his leg. His hands found her breasts before his mouth did and his breathing came up hot and shallow. Both hands roamed the land and then he penetrated. Forty minutes later they both break apart and try to catch their breaths.

"That should last you 24 hours," he said.

"24 minutes, you mean," she replied with mischief in her eyes.

"Oh. You are that riled up?"

"It's your fault for being busy. Do you know how long I had to wait? All the long nights I endured?"

"I am sorry," he said between breaths. "The office has been crazy. The Blackstone account is taking every bit of strength I have."

She rolled her eyes. "Is that why you are tired after this warm booting?"

"You know. Anyway, how is the store?"

"You want to talk business now?"

"Of course, it is allowed while we rest."

"Things have been slow for two weeks now, although it has picked up for the past two days and we have been seeing more sales. I am thinking of diversifying by bringing in different goods from our already established brands."

"Have you tested any product?"

"Well, John suggested we try our hands-on plugins."

"Isn't that too broad for a niche?"

"Oh! Sorry. Music plugins. It's all the rave these days with techno music and all that on the high rise. I care very little for those because I am not emotionally vested in them but according to his estimates we would see a sharp rise once we get that rolling."

"I think I agree with him. Most kids are into music production. The advent of electronics has changed the way music is being perceived. Sinatra started all this and now it is quite possible to do incredible things with these tools. Things that don't even make sense acoustically in the real world."

"You seem to know a lot about this thing. Are you the corporate Tony I know?"

"I used to be in a band during college. I somehow kept up with the growing trends just for the sake of my sanity. My work schedule doesn't afford me the time to make music so I have to live vicariously through these youths."

"This is all surprising to me."

"I have more surprises for you tonight. If you know what I mean."

"I like that kind of surprise." She drew in and kissed him then went to the bathroom.

The knock on the door surprised Tony.

"Princess?"

"Yes!"

"Did you order anything?"

"No. Why?"

"Because there is someone at the... Never mind." He got off the bed and fished for his trousers. He was still buckling his trousers when the knock came again. This time louder and more insistent. Tony wondered who it was. Princess appeared behind him with a towel over the towers. What met Tony's eyes when he opened the door was none other than his wife, Star.

"What are you doing here?" he managed.

"I can ask you the same thing." She pushed past him and stopped dead in her tracks when she saw Princess.

"Hello, Star," Princess said in a condescending tone. Both women stared at each other.

"How is this possible?" Star asked no one in particular.

Princess shrugged and went back to the bathroom. She securely locked it before sitting on the toilet. Star turned around and faced Tony. He wished the earth would grow a mouth and a hunger for him. No such thing happened.

"What are you doing here?" he asked her again.

"Is that the best you can do? I catch you with another woman and you ask what I am doing here?"

"Well, answer the question then?"

"I should be the one mad here. Why are you acting like I am the unfaithful one?"

"I never said you were anything. Why are you here?" he said it slowly, emphasizing each word.

"It got in my head that what you were saying and other things didn't tally, so I followed you here."

"And?" Star's anger jumped a rung.

"What do you mean *and*?"

"You have a problem with English? Now that you are here then what?"

She looked at him then at the bathroom door. Tony moved onto her path before her decision was made.

"Move."

"I will not."

"The whore in there is the reason you have been lying to me and neglecting your duties."

"Don't be stupid. I have lied to you but I have never shirked my duties."

"What does this mean for us?"

"I don't know." It was obvious he did, but he wanted her to say it.

"Tony, you can't do this to us."

"What am I doing exactly?"

"This!" she gestured at the room, bed and bathroom.

"We can leave here and work everything out and I would forget all this."

"How kind of you."

"I don't understand why you are being like this. Is it something I did?"

"Oh? You have no idea?" Tony walked to the bathroom door and knocked. "Come out, love." The knob turned and Princess came out nude. Star's breathing catches and she stares at both of them.

"Is this how you want to end us, Tony?"

"You mean like you planned to leave me for her?"

Silence ate all the words in the room.

"Oh. You have no words now?" Tony continued. His eyes had turned steel black. "I stumbled on your diary and saw everything. I didn't want to believe it when Princess told me about your affair. At least a woman values me as a man."

"Whatever she told you is a lie?"

Tony and Princess laughed.

"Stop making a fool of yourself, Star," Princess sneered. "It is pitiful to see you in this way."

"But... but you said you loved me."

"And I do. But I love Tony more. I have no idea why you would have this hunk of a man at home and still come to me. I will never understand women."

"Tony, please don't do this."

"What am I supposed to not do?"

"I am sorry. Please, don't do this. Can't you see she is trying to separate us?"

"How is this different from what you planned to do? I read every single entry. You even went graphic with details about your *sexcapades* with Princess. Tell me you have a book that contains mind-blowing description of our sex life."
She fell silent.
"There isn't is there? You were contemplating leaving me with the kids. If you had thought about taking the kids, I would not be this upset. But your plan was to dump us all and go partying and hitting orgasmic highs."
"That is enough, baby," Princess said as she planted a kiss on Tony's cheek. Star made a run

at her but Tony stopped her. Her hands stayed in his like a helpless child and the tremors ran to her core. She was visibly mad and animal-like.

"I will kill you, Princess! I will definitely kill you."

Princess pretended to be scared then began to tease me.

"Kill me? For what reason? You were going to leave him and the children all I did was step in."

"You deceived me!" yelled Star. "If I had known…" Tony's voice cut off her lamentation.

"What would have happened? You think it didn't hurt me to see what you wrote? To know that you were trying out different things? Didn't we agree to talk about things, no matter how complicated it was? Didn't we? You wanted to leave me because you have found love. But, it is ironic that your love has found love in me."

"She doesn't love you!"

"You will say anything because you are hurt, won't you? Just let this be. You have lost him and I have gained." Princess' words stung. It added salt to an already open wound. How did this happen? This wasn't how she had planned it all. How did this flip against her? She was sure Princess didn't love Tony. But how could she prove it? Is there any way to help him see that what she is professing isn't love?

"If you are going to leave me, please do it with another person. Please not her."

"Because you love her."

She swallowed hard. That was part of the problem but it wasn't major. Princess was a succubus, she was sure of this. What she professed wasn't love.

"Because I love you and she doesn't."

Tony froze. Princess laughed hard.

"Nice try," she said. "You really can't let this matter go, can you?"

"Shut up, Princess. I was talking to my husband." She looked at Tony's contorted face. He was thinking. "I know the sex is awesome and she makes you like you are a king and– "

"Leave."

His words cut down all her protests at the knees. The words in her mouth came out as a long sigh. She watched them go to bed and start to kiss and touch. The tears flooded her eyes making her sight blurry. Like a beaten dog, Star retreated out of the hotel room. If she stayed any longer she couldn't unsee what was about to happen.

TAMMY'S TURN

Tammy was in a spacious well-lit room. Everything was at the level of a six-star hotel, if one existed. She had returned moments ago from her spa appointment and the scent of mixed oils still clung tightly to her skin.

Over the course of two days, she had felt brand new. Her conversations with Chloe always pushed her in the right direction whenever she felt like she was missing it. The woman had encouraged her to be bold and fearless; therein lies the secret of everything.

She remembered her saying that it was a straight line to being a person of integrity and partaker of the fullness of life. Just think of the right thing to do then do it. Leave no space for comparison; just do and do it swiftly.

She still cannot believe half the things that were available in this city. Her assigned concierge had listened to her carefully. Asked about her fantasies and listened even more carefully. At first, she was shy about speaking about things that went bump in her world but the more she spoke to him the less she noticed the difference in his physique with a typical human. He had shown her different facilities with machines that would cater to different tastes.

Thinking about it still made her excited. Her schedule ran long since the first day and she dreaded the day she would have to go back to the real world.

"Whatever your fantasies are," he had said with a flourish. "They will all be fulfilled so long as you live by the rules of love and respect while you are here in the Big City of Love. You must treat everyone you meet with grace and your words must be seasoned and full of candor. Nothing else will do."

"How does everything… what sustains all this?"

"Well, the history books tell us that when the founders came here there was nothing save for the withered tree of life. They didn't know at the time that the ground they stood on was the very same place that had held the tree. For as long as time existed, the tree had served the purpose of an umbrella for mankind's sorrows. It gives and keeps on giving without complain. Broken hearts, souls that needed healing and rejects gathered to its bosom and sought succor."

She had listened to his story with rapt attention. It made little sense no matter how she flipped the story, no matter what angle she looked at it from.

But she felt happy to be here. To experience all she had so far. Quickly, she opened the closet and thought about a dress she wanted, almost immediately it appeared. She giggled like a school girl. Zo-wee, her guide had taught her how to use the facilities embedded in every building. At first, she was confused by the concept.

"How does a closet operate based on thought?

Are you playing with me right now?" His staccato laugh made her insides squirm.

"I kid you not," he had said. "This is one of the concepts that beguile almost everyone that comes here. Believe me, I have tried to become familiar with the reaction but it still is impossible for me. Follow me."

They walked a short distance to a bank of elevators.

"Now watch this." They stared but the doors didn't open, then he went close and their lips came apart. Tammy laughed.

"But that proves nothing. There are doors back in the real world that operate using sensors. So, what you just showed me isn't surprising."

"Who said I was done?" He stepped into the elevator. The floor dinged and he vanished. Tammy stayed open mouthed until the doors closed, and another on her right opened up. Zo-wee stepped out with a mischievous grin.

"Elevators in the real world do that too?"

"How did you do that?!"

"I can teach you."

"Please do."

"It may be hard for you because you haven't been to the upper floors so you have no image to draw from."

"Teach me!"

"Alright. I have an idea." His smile was beautiful.

"When you approach an elevator, think of where you want to go. For this exercise, I would like you to draw up your memory from when you were with Chloe. That should be easy since it just happened and the sensations are still fresh in your mind."

"Think of Chloe. Got it."

"Wait, you have to feel it strongly. Don't let the image waver for a moment. It would take some getting used to but it becomes easier and faster."

Tammy closed her eyes. Squished them tight and willed her mind to bring forth pictures of her time with the nurse. They flowed like a carousel and she settled on one then walked to the elevator. It opened and she screamed for joy. She was about to step in when it closed.

"What happened?" she said and turned towards Zo-wee.

"You lost your destination. In your excitement, you forgot where you were going. Try again."

She did. Then got on. Moments later the doors opened and she hopped out.

"O my God! I will never get tired of this."

"You humans are so easy to please."

"We agree!"

"Anyway, everything in its original state is powered by thought. At the speed of thought isn't a platitude cultivated by some old men in your academia. No. Everything should work like that but the systems put in place in the real world doesn't allow for this kind of movement unless when you understand a law that goes above it.

Take love for instance, there is no law above love. Love trumps everything from hate, envy, jealousy, betrayal – every negative thing you can think of is trumped by love. In the same way, if you understand what I know then traveling in this manner when I come to the real world will be no problem."

"I am a little slow from my teleportation experience. Can you explain again?"

"Maybe my analogy with love went a little over your head. Have you thought about what keeps an airplane up in the sky?"

"Not really."

"Hmm. Everyone knows that gravity is supposed to act on a body. It is because of gravity that you stand on two feet. It is because of gravity that you can jump and return to the same position. It is because of gravity that you have the concept of weight. So, how does a plane fly without being affected by gravity?"

"I don't know. It cheats?"

"Precisely."

"I just said that," Tammy said with a bewildered expression. "I didn't really think through so I am lost."

Zo-wee laughed softly. "Consider the size of the plane and its ability to convey people. The Wright brothers did not foresee this, although, one may argue on that point. Anyway, the plane uses a different law to sustain it during flight. Gravity is still acting on it in a way but a higher law is in effect so the plane stays up in the sky. I wouldn't want to go into the law of thermodynamics and all that complicated physics but," he paused.

"Please don't."

"My point is when the plane is grounded, gravity acts on it. While it was trying to take off, gravity acts on it. So, for a long time no one could figure out how to fly. It seemed impossible! I mean, think of it. Man flying? The idea was preposterous. But it all made sense when they discovered that there was another law present in the skies and if they could successfully switch realms or laws, if you will, everything would work out fine."

"So... thought is a higher realm than action?"

"Thought is action. Humans think what exists in their heads is of little consequence. But from our standpoint, thought is everything. Every created thing started as a thing. The things that exist now were only imaginations of the creator at a point in time.

Everything was called into being by the simple action of thought. Thought resounds through space. Have you heard the saying, as a man thinks so is he?"

"Many times. But I never gave it serious thought."

"There you go again. Thought. If you had paid it mind you would have gone to great lengths to dig out its meaning. Why? Because you wanted to know. But how did it all start?"

"With my thinking about it."

"Bingo."

"So how does this help me?"

"I am sure Chloe must have told you to think of what is good and act on it."

"Yes, she has." Tammy's eyes went wide with realization. She finally understood what they meant; how everything tied together to form a cohesive whole.

"My thinking shapes the kind of future I want. I have been in a place of stagnation because I couldn't envision myself move further. It wasn't the death of Michael that kept me grounded. It was my thinking about it. I feel my mind opening. It feels like walls are falling and a gust of wind is moving through my being."

"You have broken a level of enlightenment. Every happy thing is amplified here so it is easy for you to feel it intensely. Your mind just dropped the chains that had been strangling it and for once in a long time it senses freedom. We are all free to struggle but we are not struggling to be free. Once you realize that your thought can be a prison and free hall pass, life takes on new color."

"I feel so light, Zo-wee. I still can't believe the things I am feeling within me. Is it always going to be like this?"

"Not always. You will grow accustomed to this freedom and enlightenment that love brings. But unlike the average human who understands nothing, you would not grow familiar with this gift. Unless, if you forget everything you have been through thus far."

"Is that even possible?"

"Nothing is impossible. With the right knowledge and application, everything can be accomplished. Come now, we need to go tour the rest of the facility."

The ring on the door ended her recollection.

"Who is there?" she said before realizing who it would be.

"Room service," replied the voice. "Zo-wee asked that you be reminded of the dance at the big theatre. He says to not be late."

"Thank you." She called back "Tell him I will be there soon."

"Will do. Don't hesitate to send me a message if you need something. My name is Jaqua."

"Okay, Jaqua. Will do that." Zo-wee had taught her to send messages to people by using their names. It did not matter if you know a person facially or not. Using a person's name was more effective and swift.

Maybe she would get a chance to try this out before the night winds down. Right now, thoughts of dancing circled her mind. She hadn't been to a party in a long while. The last time was with Michael, and they had stayed up way into the morning.

It was only when the first shafts of sunlight were peeking through the dyed-blue that sleep came for its toll. They had slept in each other's arms like they always did. The Big City of Love was giving her another opportunity to recoup and get her energy up and she would take them on their offer.

In two days, she would return to normal life as a changed woman. She wondered if people would immediately notice the change in her or it would take some time. Tammy thought about her children glued to the television with no knowledge about where and what their mother was up to.

Her mind had been blown more than twice since she came here, and her heart seemed to be telling her it was ready to love. It was almost as if she could hear the molecular conversations between her organs and did everything feel so right. Love was in the air and breathing deeply was the best response.

TRACY

The sun was in the middle of the sky. A dim yellow ball of radiating energy. The water felt warm to her toe and Tracy adjusted the edge of her swim suit.

This was her third day in the Big City of Love and so far, every single thing was to her liking. She thought of the man that welcomed her and gave her a heart check. He was kind, not like Derek, of course Derek was kind but this one exuded it.

You could feel his kindness like tentacles. Although she had been bewildered when she found herself in a place she knew nothing about, on a queue she had no idea how she got on, the one thing that kept her grounded was the stranger's face. Oddly enough, he didn't feel like a stranger. It almost felt like they had met somewhere but her memories were rewritten.

"Too much scifi movies will do that to you," she said out loud before adjusting her oblong sunglasses. She signaled the barkeep and ordered a colorful drink. Her concierge had been kind enough to explain things to her. The concept of thought being the most valuable currency here still made her tingle with excitement. She had asked him several questions that would have been enough to drive an average person crazy. But he kept answering all her questions in a calm natured manner. She wondered if they were somehow related to the doctor that gave her the temperament test.

After her pool time, she would go over to the parking lot and take her pick of cars. It blew Tracy away to think that you could drive anything you wanted. Even if you had no experience driving, someone would teach you. The idea was totally rad.

A tall slender man walked past her with a towel and a long glass. Their drinks were of the same color. She stealthily stole a look at him and their eyes met. He smiled. She tried to apologize but the words refused to fall in line for a coherent sentence to flow.

"I am Jake," he said. She noticed his pearly whites and her heart went bungee jumping.

"I am Tracy." She cussed herself for stammering.

"Nice to meet you, Tracy. Where are you from?"

"Uhmm… Is it okay to talk about where we come from? I think there is a rule against that?"

"Not really? When people are interested in each other that rule fizzles away." He gave her a wink. She did not catch on.

"I am from a cold place with a lot of French fries," she said with a grin.

"That wasn't vague at all but I will follow your cue. I am from a place with tricycles and festivals."

"Easy! You're from India."

"Ha! That is a generalized way of seeing things. What if it was Africa?"

"But it isn't. Tricycles are fairly recent in Africa. Almost everyone with a VCR knows that tricycles and pull carts are associated with India. But I don't mean that in a derogatory way."

"I am not offended by your statement," he said and took a sip from his glass. Slowly, he walked over to her and gestured.
"Do you mind if I sit by your side?" A part of her wanted to scream about the hots she was getting from him. The other part dominated and forced her to act cool.

"Sure," she gushed and adjusted. "Why not?"

"Thank you." He smelled of autumn leaves and too much confidence. Tracy never knew such a scent could turn her right up to the clouds.

"How did you get here?" Asking him questions would be the only way she could survive the rising tide hitting against her chest.

"Long story! I would feel stupid saying it."

"It's a good thing we have time and a very good barkeep."

"You ever consider a career in law or politics?"

"Teaching suits me just fine."

"Oh. You are a stellar model to the younger generation. I always say people fail to recognize the role of teachers in society."

"I would totally agree with you if you weren't trying to dodge the story of how you got here." His laugh came out dry.

"I honestly wasn't. Talking about education is more interesting to me than all the things that are above my head."

It was her turn to laugh. So even this intelligent looking man found The Big City of Love too large a concept to wrap his head around.

"Are you an educator?"

"I dabble," he said. "I am in academia but most times I would rather travel and be loose than tied to a desk. I understand the plight of the teachers though."

"Never end a sentence with though."

"I used it colloquially. Speaking this way is a parlance I learned from social media and hanging with youths too young to be my close friends."

"Spoken like a social scientist."

His smile caused his eyes to close.

"An observer, you are. I am a social science major and I enjoy the little pleasure of learning from people that aren't my peers. Staying relatable and relevant is a skill that is being lost by many in the field."

"You all read too many texts and become old and boring."

"It is a curse we are yet to find deliverance for, I'm afraid."

"I get that. I sometimes have to deal with parents that don't get their children. They have this conceived notion that the path that worked for them in bygone years should be the same for their seed."

"It's an archaic form of thinking and I am surprised that it still shows up in the educational sector. But what I find interesting is your use of seed when the usage of that word in the context you portrayed is all but forgotten."

"That was a joke." Tracy giggled. "I like doing that in the hope that someone would catch on."

"Well, I did. And I demand a reward."

"The day is still young, you may yet a reward."

"I look forward to it. So, what grade do you handle?"

"The easily impressionable and up and coming."

"That is a vague but wide gamut."

"I do teens and preteens. The school I handle has a system of pairing you with a class you have built a bond with. So, I have been with my students for some years now."

"Interesting. Is that the same system where you teach them everything?"

"Oh. You are knowledgeable. It is similar to that but I don't handle everything per se. Just sometimes. But for the most part, I do."

"Doesn't that get too stressful for you? I mean, we are talking about every single subject."

"It doesn't. I know it sounds weird to most people when I say that but it really doesn't. I love to read, teach and experiment with things. Becoming a teacher was a logical step I did not see at first. I had wanted to be a research assistant or something cool like that. Now, I am resigned to the fact that teaching brings me joy and my dancing covers for the adventure I lack."

"You dance? Professionally?"

"You sound surprised."

"I am. I didn't peg you for a dancer." He said the word dancer using a British accent.

"It isn't anything fancy like that. I wouldn't say professional but I am an exotic dancer. I was at work when I came here."

"Where you in full costume?"

"Sexual harassment is still a crime, you know." They both laugh.

"I wasn't to get into... stop making me think about it. It's hard enough having you close to me."

"You can always go back to your recliner. What is that saying about heat and staying out of kitchens again?"

"Don't start a volcano in a closed space, do it outside?"

"That is not the one."

"Well that is the one I know."

"Too bad."

He takes a deep breath and runs a hand through his hair. "I was at a strip club when I got swallowed here. My pants were down and I saw bright lights all around me." He stared into the blue pool and cleared his throat. "My ex-girlfriend had brought me to the court to be judged. At first, I didn't understand what was happening until I started to hear all I had done. It wasn't like I had planned to hurt anyone but my heart just couldn't take anything serious and I left a series of broken hearts and tears. Jane was the one person I thought I could build with… in the end I still I treated her like a disease and went back to my life of neon."

"I am so sorry to hear that." Tracy didn't have the words that would comfort this grieving person. She wasn't sure the words she wanted to speak would even make a dent on the way he felt.

"It's quite alright now. We somehow straightened things out. I don't even know why I am telling you this, maybe it's because you are easy to talk to."

"I don't think I am, but I don't take lightly the fact that you are open with your personal struggles."

"So, what happened to uh…"

"Jane? Oh. I apologized and all that. She had met someone and gotten married to him but she couldn't move on because of the way things were left between us."

"Excuse my curiosity when you are grieving, but did you say court?"

He looked at her like she had two heads. "Yes. I am surprised that a lot of people don't know about the court. The people I met kept telling me they found themselves on a line and then they were taken to a room and some tests were done on their hearts. The temperament check I understand; I had gone through the same process after the court proceeding. You are the fifth person to not know there is a court here."

"My concierge never mentioned this."

"This is strange. Do you think there are different reasons as to why we are here? I cannot understand why I went through a court while others found themselves on a line."

"I too was on a line," Tracy declared. "A man with blazing light approached me and took me through the emergency doors. He explained things to me before taking me for a heart check. Wait, maybe your case is different."

"Maybe."

"Well, there is no use thinking about it. We can ask my concierge or yours when they come to get us for the party later. You are coming right?"

"Only if you would be my date."

"I don't drink cheap wine. It makes me throw up."

"Then it is a good thing that money isn't a problem and I know how to show a girl a good time."

"Don't overestimate yourself. You may still fail."

"What else does a man have other than confidence in himself?"

"A step down the over confidence ladder might do him good."

"But you don't like that type. You like us confident but not arrogant and I am a perfect blend of these worlds."

Tracy did not say anything. She gingerly dropped her towel and dived into the warm water. It accepted her then let her float before she flipped on her back. No one asked Jake to get into the water. He knew that was an invitation and a dare. He took a deep breath and plunged in like a nuke. Gracefully, Jake swam to where she was and kissed her full on the mouth before diving deeper into the water. Tracy followed with a curios smile plastered on her face.

T.J LOSES EVERYTHING

T.J still hated looking at himself in the mirror. Yet he always did. Tomorrow would be his third surgery but to him, nothing had changed. He had become the ugly duckling and thoughts of suicide hung over him like a halo. He felt broken, depressed and hopeless. He felt abandoned – none of his friends had come to visit him.

His fame, great looks and money were gone – and he was all alone. He raised his hand and felt the mass of congregating dead skin on his face.

The cops had caught up with Sandra in Santa Barbara. She was living in a dirty motel with a boyfriend that was believed to be the mastermind behind all her actions. T.J asked that no information be given to him regarding the matter. Sandra was dead to him and he hated constant reminders of the inexcusable and heartless action she had taken against him. The burn wounds were already enough to last him a lifetime.

The nurse in charge of him rolled him out in a wheelchair to go get some sun. It was hot outside but the breeze made it nice and bearable. T.J was permanently scarred for life. He had endured 3 unsuccessful surgeries and soon realized that his acting and modelling career was over. He wanted to die; he felt that his life had no further purpose.

"Do you like it here?" He turned and for the first time noticed her beauty. She was a beautiful brown islander with the clearest skin he had ever seen. She was in her mid-30's and appeared well educated. T.J was intrigued by her level of professionalism and presumed she was here because the family was in financial ruin. Why else will someone as young as she be working in a rehabilitation facility?

"Would you like living in hell?" he replied.

"She giggled and replied, I didn't mean it like that." I am here to help you recover, it is going to be fine. "I meant it like that."

"The matron said you used to be a famous actor and model. What was it like?"

"Emphasis on used to."

"Yes, but what was it like? Is it as glamorous as tv paints it? My ma says everything the media shows is a lie and a fabrication."

"That is a good way to put it."

158

"So? Is it true?"

"What?"

"The media."

"What is wrong with the media?"

"Mr. T.J, sir."

"Call me Terrance."

"But everyone calls you T.J."

"Is your name everyone?"

"No. My name is." He cut her off.

"I am not interested in your name."

"Why do you have to be so mean?"

"Why do you have to try to make me remember what I am forgetting?"

"That sentence isn't right"

"Now you want to be my English tutor also. I must be cursed."

"Why say something so morose?"

"Morose?"

"It means showing ill humor."

"Did you cram that while in high school? How old are you anyway?"

"Why?"

"I need the information to win the lottery." Silence. "I have been contemplating and it would go until I find an answer so please?"

"I am 35," she said with a smile.

"You fib!"

"But I have no reason to lie to you."

"Yea, because I am no longer a handsome devil."

"I don't know anything about devils but you are handsome enough in my book."

T.J sharply raised his head to look at her.

"You don't know what you are saying."

"I don't? Are you trying to change what I consider beautiful, good sir?"

"Anyone told you that you can be annoying?"

"Every single day! My mother is a school teacher and my dad is a novelist. They both agree that I am headstrong and plenty annoying. I never let it bother me though because I know they love me terribly. So why do you think you are cursed?"

"Add nosey to that list." She giggled.

"That was the first time I have seen you smile since I got here."

"There is nothing to smile about. My looks are gone. My house. Car and even my friends. I tried calling them but all I get is their voicemail. None of them have set foot here since I was admitted. The ones I luckily got through to, gave me one excuse after another. They have all abandoned me." His body vibrated.

"But I have not!"

"You don't count."

"That was hurtful. If I didn't think you were being cute, I would be upset."

"Stop saying I am cute. Stop telling me lies."

"You are really stubborn, T.J."

"Do your job and wheel me in, will you? The sun is enough for today."

...

In his room, T.J found himself replaying everything the strange lady had said. There was no way she could think of him as handsome. Absolutely no way! He had nothing to give her. Maybe she was fixated on his past achievements. But they weren't much, to be honest.

He lied about most of the jobs he got; it was just the way of the world he lived in. He thought about all the beautiful women he had in his bed. The way he made all the pretty women jump and shout whenever he was around. Now? None of those women would even look his way.

His loins ached for just one to look his way, to at least come visit. But he knew it was too much to ask, it was too much to wish for. Sandra had done irreparable damage to his heart and he felt hurt and betrayed. Suicide was the only option. The management knew there were times of depression so they built and furnished the facility in a way that didn't give any opportunity for one to kill, let alone harm themselves.

T.J was contemplating this when he saw himself in a long queue. As far as his eyes could see on both sides people were coming and going from a huge dome seated in the middle. Inside, he was blown away by the architecture and latticework done on the place. There was a large heart-shaped device in the center of the building and he saw people being attended to. First, a heart attached to their arm is removed then they are taken to a room.

"Hello, T.J. I am Can-Du," said a tall man in a white suit and gelled hair. I am sure you have questions. I am here to answer them."

"Where am I?"

Keep your head up, everything is going to be fine. T.J said, "have you seen me! Look at me! My life is over!"

Can-Du replied, there is no need to be down. He told T.J to look down at himself. As TJ's eyes glazed downward he was in disbelief. His body had been restored to its natural state. No burn wounds or disfigurations were visible – he was that tall, dark and handsome actor and model again. He was dressed in his fashionable attire and he had his confidence back. T.J jumped up

163

from the wheelchair and realized that he could walk again.

"What is happening to me?" "How did you do that?" "Where are we?" T.J asked.

"You are in the Big City of Love. There is no judgment, no negative energy here! Walk with me."

T.J followed him without question, and they took an elevator to the highest point of the building. They got out and rounded a hall then entered a room that looked like a Skybox at a sports arena. They could see and hear everything going on below.

"Down below is the Court of Love. Sit back and watch and I will explain why you are here later.

We have two cases to see here before we move on. They have already begun...shhhh!"

T.J watched what was happening below them. He could hear everything inside his head. It was weird at the onset, being on this side, that is. There was a man and a woman pointing an accusatory finger at a woman in the middle of the courtroom. The two were on an elevated platform while the woman stood on a slightly depressed ground. Suddenly, bright lights shone, and T.J caught movement above.

"What is that," he asked Can-Du

Amused, Can-Du answered, "That is the Judge of this place. He handles everything especially when it comes to court cases."

"He is big!"

"Yes. He judges, while the two that are invisible right now, are guardians of the court."

Can-Du was not assigned to T.J previously, so he was not aware at that time that T.J had been summoned before. He went on to explain to T.J how individuals get to the Court of Love. When you break so many hearts you get summoned by them.

At first, you get a warning, this manifests as an unsettling feeling in your gut. The feeling persists if the heartbreaker does not amend their ways. Remember when you were uneasy about hurting Natalie?" T.J pretended not to have heard him.

"Princess, do you know where you are?" the Judge asked.

"No."

"You have been weighed and found wanting. These two had love and you sought to steal and separate them from each other. When Star found her way to this sanctuary she gave your name as the cause of all her sorrow and pain. This isn't your first time breaking up love, for the sake of your selfish need.

In the past, you have been summoned here before and you know our ways, yet you pretended that none of this looked familiar to you. How do you plead to the charges brought against you?"

Princess looked around with disdain. "It is natural for a woman to see what she wants and go get it. What is wrong with that? I have always done what my natural instincts pointed me towards. Isn't that what you teach here? Isn't this place a philosophical cesspool of motivation and doing what is right? Tony felt right for me. Yes, he did. How is taking him away from her a crime?

She had no idea about what she wanted. Why should my realization and pursuit of something desirable now become an offense? This court is a sham! You asked if I am guilty or not guilty. You are doing it wrong. These two are weak and don't belong together. Tony is mine! Star doesn't love him as much as I do. She wanted to leave him to be with me. Why isn't she on trial? I love Tony.

I am willing to take on all the responsibility she has been skimping on all this time. But no, no one sees the effort I have put into this. She is the victim and I am the thief that came in the night when she wasn't properly minding the love put in front of her."

"Because I realized my mistake. I realized my sin and I went back to my love."

"I realized that she was all I wanted," Tony added. "I realized my sin and I went back to my love. All I ever wanted was Star, but we grew apart because we were both preoccupied with work. You were supposed to be our counsellor. You were supposed to give us advise on how to restore the love that had grown thin, but instead you took her away from me. Then you tried to take me away from her. How do you sleep at night?"

"But, Tony, you love me. All those times we spent in each other's warm embrace meant nothing to you? Are you going to throw what we started to build because she shed tears and flashed you some skin? Don't be deceived! She doesn't want any part of you. Why else would she abandon the children you brought into this world? She was ready to cut any and all ties to you. Yes, she labored and pushed them out of her womb but who in their right minds will leave the children she toiled so hard to bring forth? You think she loves you? You think all this is remorse and repentance? It is a charade. She will repeat the same thing if given the chance. Tony, leave this woman and come with me. I will remain faithful to you. I will let you have my body without reserve. I will stroke your ego without shame. What we have is true and powerful. Everything you had with her has waned, there is no longer life when your eyes meet."

Star spoke out with a shout. "Stop saying those things! When I came to you with my pain about how distant we had grown, you started sowing a seed of doubt within me. I regret to say this, but you tempted me and I foolishly followed"

"Someone had to!" Princess replied with a laugh.

"Just one look at Tony when he came to get you and I knew you were the most foolish woman on the planet. Why would you be blind to the treasure in front of you? The man dotes on you despite his busy schedule. He is one of the few remaining that cherish marital commitment and the trappings that come with it. You were complaining about not getting enough sex when you could not see that the man was going through stuff and he needed you to lean on. You were and still are self-centered. How you got married to him still baffles me. Tony is beyond you. You don't deserve him. I know this. You know this. He knows this. Go ahead. Tell her what you told me during one our sessions."

Tony bowed his head. "Don't be docile now. Tell her what you had told me. Let her see the man she had been blind to all this while. Break free of the shackles of sensitivity and always trying to be good natured. She is right there, Tony. Why don't you tell her how much she has hurt you? You listened back to our conversations, did you not?

You even went through her diary. Why then do you hesitate. Tell her! Speak!"

"There is nothing to say. I cannot claim to have love if I cannot forgive. I cannot claim to have love if I hate my fellow brother. All you have said is true. Star has hurt me more times than I can count but I cannot leave her because I have vowed to stay with her. She is the mother of my children and the woman I have loved for as long as I can remember. What I feel for you is strong- it was strong while Star was not occupying my vision but now I see differently.

How am I supposed to stand before our children and explain to them the reason their mother would no longer be coming home? I grew up in a broken home. It would be unwise of me to subject my children to the same treatment. Can you not see that she is sorry for all she has done? You are our counsellor, why can't you do your job and be happy for us? File our case under your success story and move on."

"I cannot do that because of what I feel for you, Tony. You think I wanted to play the part of the person that breaks a home – yes, I wanted to. I cannot even lie about that anymore. I wanted to break you up so bad because I wanted you. The feeling I got when you finally looked at me like a woman goes beyond words. I wanted you because I am the only person that can love you the way you deserve. I understand you, Tony. Let us blow this court and go eat more fruit from our love garden. This is a sham. They don't understand our love; ours is a love born out of circumstances that were unfavorable. This is the strongest type of love available but this court would not see it as so. You, what are you doing? Tell him you don't want him anymore so that he wouldn't feel guilty."

"I cannot do that," Star said through sobs. "You made me… it is childish to not take responsibility

170

for one's actions so I would say, it was my fault. I wanted to see what bi-sexuality entailed and you gladly showed me the ropes. I was blinded for a time but now I see things clearly. I will always love, Tony. He is the only man for me. He is the only sexual orientation I need."

"And I will always love you, Star. You make me complete. You are the light that graces my darkened clouds. You give me strength each morning. You are the reason I want to wake up each day and go to work. I am sorry for any pain I may have caused you. I am glad for this opportunity to return back to you, my first love. You are the world to me. You mean everything."

"You both make me sick. You sound like robots! Tony, come away with me. I am the only one that can make you happy, baby. Please come away with me. Leave Star, she doesn't deserve this follow me. Can you hear me, Judge? Let me go away with my lover. Why won't you judge in my favor? When will this court recognize my right to love however I please? Stop poking your nose into my business!" Princess' brows knitted and her agitation rose.

There was a sound and she vanished.

"What happened?" T.J asked with fear and trepidation.

"She angered the Judge so he disintegrated her. Foolish woman. She should have begged. Such is the end of the simple. They refuse to seek wisdom so their end is pitiful. This isn't her first time here, the case is always the same. She takes from a happy couple. Or at least she tries, then we intervene."

"I felt pity for her," T.J said absentmindedly. "I kind of relate to her pain. Sometimes it's almost as if all the people you are compatible with were taken before you came on the scene."

"I get what you mean, but her case is different. She derives pleasure from breaking homes and leaving the people that were once happy wretched. It isn't her fault and for the first four times the judge flowed in the way of mercy. She has had a hard life with no love. The only love she had was tough. It is a miracle that she turned out alive with this twisted version of love she wished everyone would adopt."

"Four times? She stole husbands four times?"

"This was her eighth attempt. A rather diligent home wrecker that one. The first time she came here, I felt so much pity I was upset with the judge for not ruling in her favor. You see, although we seem to possess every conceivable piece of information, this cannot be any further from the truth. We only know about the city and the people assigned to us. The judge on the other hand, knows everything. So, I wasn't privy to the knowledge he had but I took an offensive stance. It was much later that I felt ashamed after she appeared here for the third time."

"But, if– "

"Ssh! A new case is about to commence."

The lights went off and a spotlight shone on a different woman. She was about 28 by T.J's estimation, and she was draped in fine jewelry. An elderly man is on the raised platform and he points a finger at her.

"Do you know where you are, Salome?" asked the Judge of time.

"No…" she looked around and was visibly shaken. "Where am I? Adam, is that you?"

"Yes, I have grown tired of your antics. My old heart cannot take it anymore. You keep doing things that hurt me and I have to constantly defend you. I had fallen in love with you because you understood me. You were the only person I could confide in after Maggie died, but you morphed into someone I no longer recognize."

"Who are they," asked T.J.

"The honorable judge Adam and his trophy wife, Salome. The man is in his sixties and a well-respected member of his community. Wife died ten years ago and he had been a widow until fairly recently. Salome was his secretary. They found love in the strangest of circumstances and started to go out on dates and all that stuff you humans enjoy. Most people thought they wouldn't work but somehow everything did. He promised her the world if she would marry him, I almost forgot that part. The honorable judge practically begged to have this woman become his wife. Funny thing was, she wanted to, but she felt giving in so easily would paint her as a gold digger to society. Long story short, some months into the wedding she begins to act out. This woman steals, cheats, lies and hurts the man's soul on a regular basis. It has become like clockwork; he expects trouble every time he is awake."

"Does the court handle every love case?"

"Well, it depends. Some find their way here and we have to help them, It is something that is built into the city. You can't let a broken heart wonder around and not help. It is not how we do things."

"You are in the court of judgement of love," the judge bellowed. "You have been weighed and found wanting. Adam has accused you of infidelity and neglecting your wifely duties. How do you plead?"

"Guilty! I have been unfair and wicked to him but I did it because of the advice I was given. I take this all as my fault. Please forgive me, Adam. You know I love you. I am sorry for all the heartache I have caused you. I have been insensitive to your needs, please forgive me." Salome went down on her knees and pled for mercy.

"What advice, Salome?" Adam asked with heavy concern.

"The other women at the ball. They told me the best way to keep the judges under control is to act out. Every time I did something that brought you grief, I lost a part of me. But I had seen and heard stories of how you judges go about with different women while leaving your wives at home. I didn't want to be in that kind of marriage."

"You injure me with your words. Do I look like those kind of people? I have always told you that certain people would come between us. I told you some individuals will use your sweet innocence against you – against us. You let them win!"

"I am so sorry," Salome cried. "But I was afraid of losing you. My love for you was so strong. I reasoned if I behaved poorly then my attachment to you would grow weak and it would not hurt me if you started to behave like all the women had said you may act."

"I am shocked by this. You acted all on a probability that did not exist in my case. When have I ever given you cause to worry? Every day I try to be a better husband to you. I ask for more things that I needed to know so we can bridge the gap created by our age difference. You have never told me that you felt insecure… I assumed we were fine. I thought … it doesn't matter what I thought."

"I am sorry, gummy bear. I didn't think things through. I am a fool and I realize that now."

"There is no need for me to go down there. Her plea seems genuine enough," gushed Can-Du.

"Isn't that biased?"

"How so?"

"She may be the same as Princess or any other person that is a victim of circumstance."

"Are you inferring that her confession isn't genuine?"

"I am not inferring anything. I am saying that the course of action she took was foolish. Why follow anyone else's advice when you could easily learn who your partner is? Love is just stupid."

Can-Du looked at T.J through the corner of his eyes.

"So you have never made any mistake in your life?"

"That is absurd. Everyone has made mistakes. My point is, there are mistakes that are worth making when you look at them from hindsight. She would still feel stupid no matter how this story is flipped. She knows she has taken a path that she shouldn't have if her brain was working correctly."

"But as you said, love is stupid. Right."

T.J wet his lips before answering. He knew Can-Du was being a cynic but he didn't care. His opinion still stood. "Right."

"I am surprised that you are spouting such nonsense. You of all people ought to know and understand the power of wrong decisions and how foolish you would feel no matter what you do after you realize it was a mistake. If I take what you are saying a step further, then it translates as forgiveness should only be given to mistakes that are worthy of it."

"That too should be considered. That wasn't what I had in mind but that too should work. Forgiveness isn't something that should be offered like oxygen. No, it should not!"

"Keep your voice down. You may interrupt what is going on down there."

"Look, you expect me to forgive for what happened to me. Just look how maimed I have become. I did not do a single thing to deserve what I have gotten. Yet, you speak to me about forgiveness. Where do you get off telling me what I should give and what I should not?"

"I am not trying to be pick a fight with you."

"I could have sworn that was your intention."

"I know you are hurt."

"I am beyond hurt, grieving, pissed or whatever adjective you want to employ. I am mad. I am disappointed. Some days I wish I would die. Anything is better than what I have right now."

"That is a rather shallow way of thinking. Some people are dead and buried but you are still alive. You still have a chance at life but they have lost that shot, yet you sit here and spout nonsense. What do you know?"

"I never claimed to know much but this is *my* life. I have no future. Have you taken a long and good look at what I have become? No female will ever want me again. All the monies I paid for plastic surgery have gone down the drain of unfruitfulness. I can't stand to look at my face in the mirror yet you speak of forgiveness. The judge's wife deserves worse judgement than Princess. Her ignorance should cost her. At the rate things are going only privileged people will have good graces."

Can-Du refused to answer, instead he turned his attention back to the proceeding below. He knew he couldn't make any headway with T.J when he became like this. The man was as stubborn as a mule, maybe a Bison. Besides, this wasn't the way to heal a broken heart.

It was abundantly clear that the guy was hurting and all his points were valid. But what will become of humanity if everyone is held to the standard he was proposing? What would survive in a world without forgiveness? Hell would be better.

A light filled the room, Adam and his wife were taken out unconscious on a stretcher. The judge had decided the couple needed therapy so the emergency heart center would be the place to go. Can-Du should be in charge of this because it seems like something only he would be capable of. Plus, there was the matter of Zo-wee being away and Can-Du being assigned to T.J.

"Where are they taking them?" T.J asked.

"To the emergency room where their hearts would be fixed and put back in order. There is a machine responsible for weighing how far gone a person's heart was. Here in the city, everything was done in peace and order. There is no force involved. The big guy wants to talk to you."

"Huh?"

"Why do you think you are here? Once every century, a man is chosen to come see the Big City of Love. He is granted access and gets to become an ambassador. Turns out your mother's dying wish was for you to find love. It took this long but you are finally here. This is all too heavy."

Can-Du laughed. "The judge will be here shortly to explain everything to you."

Light filled the room then concentrated into a small ball in front of T.J. Slowly it morphed into a human form with white short hair.

"I am the judge of night, day and the love that falls liquid," he began in a resounding voice, "I am the first concierge and guardian of secrets in this city flowing with love. You have met third generation creation, Mike-kee. Zo-wee will join you later on the tour. Can-Du is in charge of the entire city and has been assigned to the couple you just witnessed. Although the Big City of Love is magical, at its core is the energy of healing. Healing permeates this city and is weaved, even at this moment throughout every cell. This city was built on land that was once home to the tree of life. For eons, nothing occupied this land except for the tree of life. Because of its unmatched energy, nothing else could cohabit with it. The tree of life was an everlasting giver of life and love. It was an oasis for the broken hearted and a source of healing to the weary. It was a magical dwelling for hearts and souls in need of healing. People came in from all over the world to touch, to sit under or just to get close to the tree of life. For centuries people all over the world have somehow found themselves at the mercy of the tree of life. Learning the true meaning of forgiveness, love, self-respect, and self-confidence. Restoring their self-confidence. Giving them a renewing spirit of forgiveness and understanding ultimately leading to self-love which allows them to confidently love again in the path of greatness. Your mother came here shortly after this dome was built. They were having trouble with your father. You were too young to remember this. I heard her dying wish and decided you would be an ambassador just like Can-Du. But first, we need to get your heart in order."

"You think feeding me some mysterious tale is enough for me to follow you or let you do anything to me? You must be on a really cheap drug." The judge laughed. His laughter was soft, liquid and easy on the ear.

"I know everything about you but it hasn't prepared me for meeting you face-to-face. Boy, are you a riot. I understand that Sandra's action still hurts you and the fact that your burn wounds have left you scarred for life but there is still a way for you to live happily."

"Let me guess, forgiveness."

"You make it sound like the ugliest thing in the world."

"Well, I don't consider it beautiful. I see no reason for this conversation. There is absolutely no point."

"Sure, there is, your heart is the point we are after. This woman has broken your ability to receive and transmit love. She has taken you and turned you inside out and the pain is still raw. I understand all too well."

"Have you been burned before?"

"No, but I feel your pain. It isn't empathy. I am connected to you as much you are connected to me. The only difference is that I can feel what you feel but you have not been trained to feel what I feel or any other person's feeling for that matter."

"Easy for you to say. You weren't the one that gave all they had and still got burned in the process. What use is there to get serious with love when this is all you would get? I thought she was the one. I thought it was the us against the world but it wasn't so, I was just a plaything." He broke down and the tears flowed freely down his cheeks. T.J's body shook with anger and pent up frustration.

Judgment for Sandra

Sandra was summoned to the Courts of love for judgment for all the hearts she had broken and the wrong doings in her life. Sandra received the maximum penalty of Life with "No love". The men in her life, were drawn to her innocence and seductive acts. She used them all for emotional and financial gains. She got them to fall in love with her, but because of her deeply rooted insecurities, when she felt them pulling away from her and/or showing interest in other women, she set her plan in motion to take them for everything they had worked so hard to build and leave them bankrupt and broken.

Sandra attempted to murder many of the men she had previously been involved with and succeeded with one encounter. She was not convicted in Federal Court because her well renown attorney convinced the jury that the malicious act was self-defence.

The men that Sandra hurt, including T.J and the family members of the man murdered by Sandra stood in the Courts of Love to pass judgment on her.

Sandra entered the Court heartless and unapologetic. Her scowl was blank and emotionless. She took her position in the middle of the Court wearing a bright red jumpsuit and refused to look at her victims. T.J was enraged at the sight of her but was able to maintain his composure. He replayed the conversation with the judge over and over in his head regarding forgiveness as he listened to testimonies from the men that stood with him. As the judge gave the verdict of Life with "No love", she can not fall in love and no one will ever love her again. Sandra left the court with no remorse and did not appear to be moved by the ruling.

T.J ARRIVES AT THE EMERGENCY ROOM

T.J began to daydream and fantasize about his body being healed and being normal again while the nurse was talking to him.

T.J finds himself standing in a long line. The people in line were conversing about their life –

sharing their stories with one another explaining why they are there. Some stated, I have tried to love this man and he did not love me back, I am heart broken, I never felt love before – my family never loved me, my friends never loved me…

One woman asked, Is this the place for Broken Hearts? Another woman uttered, Yes! this is the place to regain your self confidence, your self worth, and find love again. To experience this you must wait in the long lines and go through the emergency room entrance. The emergency room is in a dome shaped building with glass doors. People were so happy to be in the lines because they were looking to find love again, gain self confidence, live again, respect others …. Live, Love and Experience… that is what the City of Love gives.

T.J is admitted to the emergency room ready to have his heart mended – ready to love again.

With a rapid heartbeat, T.J walks through the emergency room doors and begins the intake process. TJ's head was foggy and he was uncertain of why he was in the emergency room.

As the nurse completes the triage on TJ, she asks "who hurt you so bad?" A puzzled T.J asks, "what do you mean?" The nurse turns to T.J with a smirk on her face and tells him based on her prognosis, his heart needs a tune up. "Your vitals are off the charts!" She exclaims.

A convicted T.J lowers his head and tells her that he wants his self-confidence back and is ready to love again.

As the nurse input notes into the computer system, she advises T.J that she can see that the lady who tried to destroy him is a Sandra Parker. TJ's heart rate rises at the sound of her name. The nurse tells T.J to remain calm. I understand where your emotion is coming from but rest assured that you will gain so much more when you are done here. She tells him that she does not believe in coincidences and that he must trust that his heartache, pain and suffering was destined to occur, but he will walk away a better man if he is willing to trust his heart. As T.J exits the triage area to return to the waiting room, he miraculously feels a glimpse of hope again.

He felt light envelope him and for a brief moment he saw the judge's face. Warmth coursed through his veins and a newness strengthened his bones.

"You will be okay," he heard the judge say before everything washed away like a canvas soaked in water.

T.J woke up to the face of the strange lady. She smiled at him and a surge of warmth flowed through his core. He knew what he saw wasn't a dream. He could see colors around her and he sensed the love she had for him.

"I don't know why you said all those things to me in the garden today. The average person would not look at me twice but here I am feeling that all you said was true."

"I am not your average person and I only say what I mean."

"My name is Terrence but people call me T.J."

She chuckled.

"My name is Janice. I came to get you to come eat."

"Never leave me, Janice." Her cheeks burned bright pink.

"Get up Romeo. You don't need to worry about that."
He saw the light around her explode into a million colors and he assured himself that everything will be fine. The guardians of the Big

City of Love were watching over him and the path of love he was taking.

Can-Du appeared in a gold robe that flowed down to the ground and then some more. Zo-wee and Mike-kee shortly followed. They are dressed in like manner. A serious look comes over Can-Du as he looks into the river before him. The waters do a dance and change into a street then a bedroom.

"Do you think he will be alright," Zo-wee asked.

Can-Du did not answer.

"Why ask such a question? You always ask the left questions. Sometimes, it's almost… is your right brain left?"

"Why wouldn't I ask? The court assistants have been trying to get his attention but somehow it keeps bouncing back and from every indication this would be something serious."

"Why get worked up then?" Mike-kee retorted.

"There is nothing this court hasn't handled before."

"This may be new." Can-Du's words cause both pseudo-humans to gasp.

"What do you mean, sir?"

"Exactly what I said," Can-Du replied. "It's like this person has another energy backing him up, but it seems like he is unaware of anything. The scouts still haven't found a way to pinpoint what the problem is." He rubbed his chin. "This is going to be a problem."

"Whatever do you mean?" The water screen before them darkened before reverting back to the clear blue it was.

SELF REFLECTION

People are just now beginning to wake up and there are strange occurrences in everyone's mind as they face a new day. Waking up they are back at their old home and not in the City. They are trying to process what has happened.

These people have spent a few days in The Big City of Love and as they awaken they are all asking themselves "was this a dream? Or was this real?"

At the moment they do not know as their mind is racing with thoughts.

If their time in The Big City was a dream but the results are real doesn't it then make the city real?

Everyone who went to the City has changed in a big way. We have featured six people, but there were more.

Due to the creation of the Big City of Love these people have changed and have a better life. They are accepting the positive results of their trip.

They realize they were sent to the City on a special mission. This City is one where one simply cannot schedule a trip and go there. One must be sent there on assignment. One cannot refuse the assignment.

The City was created in seven days. There are no storms in the City. Some may say this parallels heaven?

This City does not have religious tones, but does have moral basis for all the decisions.

This city, because it is in a dome, it has it's own perfect environment. One needs never worry if the weather will play a part to ruin their day's plans. Although, there are parts that have artificial darkness, the city itself has no night.

Why are some people called here? T.J was warned he was traveling down the wrong path and the courts had to take him to the courts of love. Many others had caused broken hearts or had been victims of such.

The City was like a dome without the dome. Once there, people did not leave until they were sent home.

Many people wonder who the judge was? Where did he come from? This fact could never be verified other than he had always been there. He almost didn't have to say anything as the room was in awe of him and his decisions were never questioned.

Many people never saw him but they respected the word of this man, or was he a man? He stood extremely tall, and was almost too shiny and marvelous to behold. He had the ability to go wherever he wanted to be at anytime, instantly. He wore a beautiful white, very white suit. He had almost invisible multiple sets of gossamer wings.

This was a beautiful city. If possible, many would love to schedule a trip there but travel arrangements were not possible for one to go there on their own.

The City Court system controlled who came and who did not come.

If this has a profound effect on the minds of those who traveled there this basically is real and not fantasy.

Why was this town created? There was a definite need for this town and their court system. It is possible our world may not grow or succeed without this.

People come to this town with great problems and leave a totally new person.

It is possible in your own mind you can create this town and get the effects of the town. Today's people may consider this a form of prayer but this town existed for the six people we will talk more about.

These six people who are waking up, will have lives that will be forever changed. They will not vividly remember their past, but will somehow subconsciously be impacted to make future decisions.

In an almost magical way, they will be guided by their experiences, which they won't even know why, they are making the right daily decisions. It's almost as if they have been given a do-over for their lives.

Is this reincarnation? Well, they didn't die, so it isn't that. It's like a fantasy life, a miraculous, too good to be true, fantasy, but somehow it is real. After they have been treated by Can-Du and the staff, they are instantly put into a deep sleep.

When they awaken from this sleep, they will have the best day ever.

THE ADAMS' FAMILY WAKES UP

The time is 6 am and the Adams' family wakes up, in each other's arms. Neither wants the magic of the moment to end, so they lie still, pretending to still be asleep.

What happened last night, and why is she even in his bed? This is unusual and totally out of character for this married couple. And yet, here they are, with no conscious memory of what happened back in The Big City of Love.

Salome sneaks out of bed, and cheerfully goes downstairs to make breakfast. She is singing and happy, as she butters the toast and makes coffee. She is trying to recall how she has seen her husband eat his eggs before. This will be her first time ever cooking for him.

Everything is different today, and they are unsure of why. Salome is in love with the judge. Somehow, she feels a mandate, to be the wife he wants her to be. She feels no pull from other past affairs, no desire to be with anyone else.

The judge is on cloud nine, and he wants to spoil this lovely lady. His heart has mended. They are giddy, as they make plans for a honeymoon in Paris. They will stay as long as they want to. No one could love one another as much as they do now. Life is good.

Salome got a phone call from a young man that she used to cavort with regularly asking if she wanted to meet him later at the club. Salome was flabbergasted, why the nerve of him to call her and ask that, she is a married woman.

Salome's memory banks had apparently been wiped clean of all this activity. She didn't even realize this. It seemed to everyone that she not only had love surgery on her heart, but she had a heart transplant.

The judge was ecstatic. He decided to take the early retirement, and enjoy his last chapter with his young bride.

Anything she wanted, he could provide. And, now he wanted to spoil her.

JIMMY'S FATE

Jimmy had been summoned to the Big City of Love to the court to see the judge. There are no records or court records, or court transcripts we can find.

We do not know what the judge or the court said to Jimmy. The fact that these records are not available, indicate that the judge may have really let Jimmy have it.

We know Jimmy's track record with people, and how he treated people. His life may have mattered. Other people's lives maybe did not matter. There are a lot of people like that in the world today. That is one purpose of the court set up, and the Big City of Love.

Without the Big City of Love and the court system, we don't think there would be a lot of hope for people like Jimmy.

As of this moment we do not know the fact any of this will have on Jimmy or any other person who faced the judge In the Big City of Love Court.

The court was designed to help people. All people. Not just the good, not just the bad but everyone. Whoever put this court system in place was a brilliant mind?

A savior of sorts was put in place to save people, and saving the world as we know it.

Jimmy is sent back to the world that he knows. The court hopes he returns a better person.

We do not know the consequences that happen if one ignores the rulings of the court.

We do not know if The Big City has a jail system. City documents do not specify that. So, it is likely that there is no jail. How then do people like Jimmy with a bad attitude become better people after their time at the court? Time will tell. We do feel the Court has a way of following peoples progress when they leave.

Jimmy wakes up back at his regular home. He feels different but doesn't at first know why. He is groggy and will take a few minutes to figure this out.

He goes into the kitchen and makes coffee and goes outside and kneels and has prayer. What? Prayer? Jimmy?

He comes back inside and goes to the refrigerator for some food and he can't see the food as the food is behind a couple cases of beer.

One by one he takes the beer cans, and in the trash they go.

A friend calls and suggests they have a few beers later, and Jimmy says no. This friend is really puzzled at this because Jimmy has never said no to beer.

With no food, Jimmy walks into town to have breakfast.

He has his usual sausage and cheese omelette and when he finishes, he leaves a $10 tip for the waitress. You should have heard the waitress. She told everyone "Jimmy has never left a tip before and did you see him pray before his meal?"

He walked past his favorite bar and the owner said "Jimmy hope to see you tonight." Jimmy replied "I have been to the Big City of Love and I am a changed person." He went on "I have no desire to drink again and my time in the Big City allowed me to learn what was causing myself and everyone else grief."

The bar owner came to Jimmy and said "Jimmy I am proud of you. I may lose you as a customer but I will not lose you as a friend."

Jimmy saw one of the girls that danced at the club and he invited her to church. She asked Jimmy "are you judging me for what I do."

Jimmy replied "I don't judge people, I love people. I learned this at the Big City of Love. I don't have to like anyone, but I must love everyone."

Jimmy told his friends that all his relationships had failed, but now and for the first time he had what it took to succeed in a relationship.

Jimmy saw another girl who was also a dancer at the club, and she told him she was having a hard time. He told her "meet me at the grocery store and I will buy you all you need."

The word was getting around town. Many people who did not like Jimmy, were now becoming his friend.

People had heard of the Big City of Love, but they didn't understand it. Jimmy was sending a great message without trying to send anything.

Jimmy passed the local church and went inside and told the pastor he wanted to recommit his life, and how could he do things to help people.

Jimmy took all the money he had and formed a city food bank that gave out groceries every other Saturday.

When this word got out many food companies were donating food to Jimmy's food bank and then they welcomed volunteers to help.

Wow. The next Saturday the line of cars for the food bank was over a mile long. Jimmy was at the front where the cars entered and he spoke to every driver that came in.

Jimmy also had a clothing drive and had a school supply drive for the kids who were needy.

Jimmy would have a meal for all the volunteers who helped him.

The lady dancers who came through the food drive were given hugs by Jimmy and no mention of former sex escapades. Jimmy was a changed man.

He wanted his life to count for something. He wanted to make a difference in other people's lives. Each day was no longer about Jimmy, but rather about the good of society.

The pastor approached Jimmy and said "I will be gone next Wednesday night, will you give the message for me?"

Jimmy said he would be glad to.

This got around town and nobody could believe this. The common thought was if Jimmy has changed, they wanted to know how they could change.

The evening came. Normally 25 people attended Wednesday night church service. Oh my!!! There were 400 people there. It was standing room only so many congregated outside with a speaker setup for them to hear.

Jimmy shared his story of how his trip to The Big City of Love helped him find God and himself.

He apologized to everyone he had done wrong. At the altar call everyone came. Jimmy was part of Salvation for many.

Then as directed by the pastor, there was a special offering for Jimmy. The money was just for him.

The offering totaled $7000. Jimmy was asked how this offering would change his life. He calmly replied "every cent of this is going to the food pantry and clothing drive."

Jimmy also started a college scholarship fund. This was called the Big City Scholarship. This was given to students who displayed and showed the town the most love.

What Jimmy said at the conclusion of his message was, everyone has faults and everyone does wrong. Everyone can change for the better and "in my case my trip to the Big City of Love changed me. Without the Big City of Love, I would hate to think where I would be today but now, I am clear on the road ahead."

One man changed the entire town and the Big City of Love changed one man.

Maybe we don't need to try and understand the Big City of Love. All we need to understand is that the City of Love works, and works for all whether you go to the Big City or not.

TRACY WAKES UP

Tracy was suddenly awakened from a deep sleep, very confused. She thought she had been in a Big hospital, and now she was waking up to being thirteen. How could this be? She shook herself, and looked around.

It was a beautiful morning, the sounds of birds singing came thru the sunshiny windows. Tracy had awakened but the night had been very stormy, so much so that she really had to gather herself.

Where was she? Well, as she looked around, she surmised that this was her bedroom, so she must be home. However, the house had a strange eerie quietness about it.

Tracy went to wash her face, and there it was, another pimple. Her thirteen-year old face had seen far beyond her share of this.

Suddenly, she remembered the previous day. Her mother had been killed in a car crash. Her dad was unknown, and now she was alone, she thought.

The telephone rang interrupting her thoughts. The voice on the other end explained that she was

Ms. Pike, a county social worker. She said that she was coming over to meet with Tracy.

Tracy rushed about to get a shower, and get dressed before Ms. Pike arrived. She didn't know why she was even coming anyhow. Tracy had learned to pretty much take care of herself always. Her mom had always worked, and Tracy had been left alone pretty much since she started school.

She knew that she was responsible for cleaning the house, doing her homework, and cooking dinner before her mom arrived from work. Tracy even signed all her papers that were sent home for her mom to sign. She never even told her mom about them.

Tracy always knew that if the school asked for money for extra-curricular activities or fees, the answer was always NO. There was no extra money for anything. She was very thankful for having food in the house, because that wasn't always a given.

She didn't have many friends, but that was ok because she didn't usually have time for them anyhow. Tracy had big plans for her future, and these all included lots of homework and extra credit assignments.

As she scurried around the living room, picking up the clutter, the knock came on the door. It was Ms. Pike.

Tracy invited Ms. Pike in, asked her to be seated. Ms. Pike asked a million questions, she wanted to know Tracy's life history. Was there a dad in the picture, how about grandparents, aunts and uncles. And why was she left all alone at home last night?

Tracy answered all Ms. Pike's questions like an adult, and then they were just staring at one another in silence. Ms. Pike seemed to be pondering her next move.

She asked Tracy to get a bag and pack some clothes and come with me. Tracy sat obstinately, not moving. Tracy said, "I'm not going anywhere until you tell me what is happening. I'm not a child that just obeys all your commands blindly. I'm almost full grown, and I can take care of myself."

Ms. Pike told her that she didn't know all the details yet, but she couldn't leave her here all alone. Suddenly, *Tracy had a feeling come over her, that she couldn't explain. It was as if someone had taken over her voice and she had to comply with Ms. Pike's wishes.*

Tracy packed several day's clothes, and a few days clothes, and her school backpack. She felt as if she was in a daze.

She locked her front door, and got into the car with Ms. Pike. Where were we going, what was happening, so many questions running through her mind.

First stop they made was the hospital morgue. Ms. Pike wanted to find out if funeral arrangements had been made. No arrangements thus far.

There was a small life insurance policy from her mom's work and this would likely all go to the funeral home.

The house was a month to month rental, and there was no savings.

Tracy had an elderly grandmother who she didn't even know. Tracy kept saying over and over to Ms. Pike, and anyone else that would listen, that she was fully capable of taking care of herself. No one would listen or take her seriously.

Tracy was taken to a group foster home, to spend the night. There were very mean kids that lived there. They had all been horrible to her at school, and now she was left amongst them to suffer God only knew what kind of treatment.

The foster mom was trying to be nice to her, but the kids were just incorrigible.

What was she to do? Tracy didn't sleep a wink

all night, she was terrified of what the mean girls would do to her as she slept.

Morning came at last, and Tracy quickly got dressed and went downstairs to the living room. The room was dimly lit, and the furniture was old. When the sunrays started peeking through the east window, she could see dust particles accenting the morning sun.

After sitting for some time, she heard an alarm clock going off. A few minutes after, she heard water running, maybe in the shower. Shortly after, the foster mom emerged from her bedroom.

She was still rubbing her eyes as she entered the living room, and was quite startled when Tracy said a cheery good morning.

The foster mom wanted to know why Tracy was up and dressed already. She walked over to her and was trying really hard to be nice to her new foster daughter.

Tracy explained that she couldn't sleep so she got up. The mom invited her into the kitchen to sit and chat while she was getting breakfast ready. She seemed really nice, so Tracy was willing to talk.

Tracy explained that although she was only thirteen, that she had been taking care of herself most of her life. She was hesitant to address her mother's death, and seemed to almost be in denial.

The foster mom, got breakfast finished and everyone was hurried off to catch the bus to school, except for Tracy. The mom told her that they needed to attend a court hearing today, to determine Tracy's immediate future.

Tracy was terrified. Up until now, it had only been her and her mom, deciding everything that happened. Now, mom was dead and strangers were trying to make decisions for her.

They arrived at the courthouse downtown, and it was so stiff and cold to her. People were smiling and saying hello, trying to be nice. Ms. Pike was there and an attorney for her and several social workers and the judge.

Her attorney never even spoke to her. While she was waiting for her turn, she observed the social workers and judge laughing and making snide remarks about dead beat parents who hadn't shown up for their kid's hearing.

Tracy was very dismayed, and had no positive expectations about her outcome. An unidentified lady was also present at the hearing. She was young, well kept, and seemed a bit out of place.

The judge called for the case of the minor child, Tracy, and she and Ms. Pike stood up. What was to happen to her, she wondered.

All the circumstances were presented to the judge by the attorney and Ms. Pike. The grandmother had not expressed interest in fostering Tracy and there were no other known possible relatives.

Ms. Pike asked the unknown young woman to come stand by them. She then explained to the court that this was Karen Thornton, a new single foster parent, who was interested in possibly fostering Tracy.

Since there didn't seem to be any other possible avenues for her, the judge approved Ms. Thornton, and the case would be reviewed in thirty days.

With court over, Tracy was told to go with Ms. Thornton. She felt suddenly like a caged animal. She couldn't do this, she thought. She would run away and just live on the street, and continue taking care of herself.

Ms. Thornton quietly put her arm around Tracy's shoulder, and calmly explained to her, the situation. She told Tracy that she wasn't sure of all the answers. She only knew that she was willing to give it a try if Tracy was.

That same feeling suddenly came over Tracy, just like when she was compelled by some force to go with Ms. Pike. She wasn't sure why, but she said yes, ok I'll try.

The next few days went by like a whirlwind and Tracy felt like she was somewhat zombie like in her movements. There was a funeral scheduled for her mom at Ms. Thornton's church. Everyone was extremely nice to her and accepted her into their church family.

After a few days, Ms. Thornton explained to Tracy that it might be time for her to return to school, and Tracy felt ready to do so.

Ms. Thornton had a job where she could work from home, and be available any time Tracy needed her.

On Saturday, Ms. Thornton announced that they were going shopping for Tracy. The clothes she had were all second-hand, and well-worn. Ms.

Thornton thought this could be a new beginning for Tracy, and new clothes might help.

Tracy was so proud of herself. She had graduated from middle school at the top of her class. Her future looked so bright and it was all because of Ms. Thornton and her guidance.

She had big plans for her future and now she could feel it within her grasp.

She wanted to be a teacher, after college. She never wanted another child to be subject to the mean treatment that she had endured. She watched as most of those girls dropped out of school, pregnant, or runaways. She took no pleasure in seeing this happen, although she would have felt justified to do so.

The following year, Tracy was adopted by Ms. Thornton, whom she now called Mama. They had a happy home, with lots of smiles and laughter.

One night, Tracy had a very bad dream. She dreamed that after her mom died, that she was forced to live on the streets. A man came to her, being nice, and promised to take care of her. All she had to do, was prostitute herself to other men and to him.

Tracy felt trapped, with no other options. She was beaten regularly, and had a very horrific life....

Suddenly she awoke, she was trembling, it was just a nightmare, but somehow it had felt so real.

Tracy went into her Mama's room, and watched her sleeping like an angel. Maybe, she was an angel, and Tracy had been her reason for being here on earth. Her life could have turned out so differently, if not for Mama.

WHAT HAPPENS TO STAR, TONY AND TAMMY?

Star awakens after her bout at The Big City of Love, with a very confused feeling. She couldn't quite describe it. She felt empty inside.

She was in her own bed at her house, and beside her, husband Tony was waking up. They had a lot to do in order to get the kids ready and off to school.

Tony, too was feeling very strange this morning. The business of the morning took over, and the school bus whisked the kids off to school.

They both had such a weird feeling, they thought maybe they should take a sick day.

What they didn't know, is that they had been judged and sentenced.

Because of her excessive disregard for breaking up families and hurting people, her sentence was the most severe.

She would never again feel any sexual attraction to anyone, male or female. She would be stuck in this marriage to raise her children and take care of Tony, without love.

She would not be allowed to leave, but she had no knowledge of this. Day after day of mundane household tasks, with no love.

Tony, on the other hand, didn't get sentenced as harshly. He had only responded to Star's indiscretions by retaliating.

When he read her diary about all the sexcapades she was having with Tammy and Princess, he couldn't let it go. He was hurt to his core.

The Court doesn't look too kindly on people misusing love and hurting people, especially when there are innocent children, who are prone to be hurt.

Therefore, Tony was sentenced, also to No Love, but only for one year. After the year was over, the case would be reviewed. He was also unaware of his final sentence.

Tammy also had children, and a now deceased husband who was faithful to her. The courts had a little tougher time with this one.

They decided that they would take away her ability to love, also, but hers was a sentence of 6 months. After this time, her case would be reviewed.

She got off pretty easy, but if she repeated this behavior, her sentence would revert to life, or in an extreme case, she would be vaporized. If this occurred, there would be no recollection of her, to anyone she knew.

WHAT HAPPENS TO TJ

Just before T.J goes to the Courts of Love to be judged by all the hearts he has broken, T.J was warned several times to change his ways to become a better person.

T.J ignored all the warnings and at that moment, because of love, he was summoned to the courts. He would be judged by all those that have claim T.J has broken their hearts!

There was not enough so sensual evidence for T.J to get the maximum penalty at the Courts of Love, so T.J instead received only six months. Six months without falling in love, or being in love, or having any kind of happiness at all, in any kind of relationship.

T.J awakened from a deep sleep, but very troubled because of what he just encountered at the Courts of Love. T.J realized that this was no ordinary dream, and there was a lot of self-reflection going on.

Things just wasn't right this time with T.J. All of a sudden, he wanted to become a better person. He wanted to change his ways. He wanted to meet different people to see if he can get a start over in relationships.

T.J knows he was headed down the wrong path and wanted to be a better person. T.J was doing a photo shoot, and asked if anyone knew where he can go and meet a different kind of woman.

After T.J was hurt by the woman that burned down his house and took his money, T.J was suicidal.

He was very depressed, he turned to drugs and alcohol. You name it, T.J even tried to go to church a couple of times. T.J said that God probably would not answer his call because of all the bad things that he has done in the past. So, T.J eventually stopped going to church.

Then T.J found himself in the rehab where he met the nurse.

When T.J finds himself at the rehab center, he doesn't know why he's there. He is very confused. He doesn't know what to do, he doesn't know what to think, he is really extremely depressed.

He does not want people to see him because of who he once was. He goes to his rehab, but no one ever notices him.

T.J enters Rehab

When T.J enters the rehab, he is broken and suicidal. He is angry, frustrated, feels alone and feels as if he has nothing to live for. He has lost his friends, fame, money, looks -he is severely burned and feels unattractive. But something inside of him, wants to be better. He feels that there is hope on the other side and feels as if he can be redeemed if he goes through the motions – if he puts in the effort. He knows that he is not going to get his looks or body back; But he is hoping to regain his confidence and independence, he wants to feel strong and confident like a man.

One day, T.J looked up and he notices his nurse for the very first time; he has been coming to rehab but never picked his head up to see anyone. He was embarrassed because of his appearance from the burns on his body. He wants to feel good about his self again. So, one day, he finally gets to talk to the nurse. He finally glances up and see his nurse and she was very nice, and from their conversations, he could tell that she was very intelligent. She told him that she would be there every time whether you like it or not to help him get through this.

T.J asked his nurse "why you?" There are so many other nurses here that can help me. The nurse said, well, I like you and your scars do not matter to me. I am here to help you and I am going to be here until you are completely healed. I don't care who you were, you are still very handsome to me.

The nurse began flirting with T.J but somehow, in his mental state, he did not even realize that she was flirting. You could say he's thinking to himself, why would she want me because of the way I look? Look at me, I have nothing to offer this woman.

The therapy sessions continued, and they became more frequent. Then one day, T.J looked at this woman, in a different way now, she seems beautiful in his eyes. She was stunning.

She was beautiful inside and out, she was educated. She was from a different country, she was an islander. She was in her mid- thirties.

She began to build T.J back up day by day. They started to cross that bridge together.

They began to explore a relationship. T.J did not want to be hurt again because he had been torn down from his mind, his skin, and his body. He just wasn't very confident at all.

He had hoped, though, that he could be redeemed and become better.

He has not always been a good person. He has used people for the moment. He felt that his world was crumbling before him. He felt that this was his Karma. He had become bitter, he had no money, no looks and nothing to offer anyone.

T.J arrives at the emergency room entrance for broken hearts…

T.J began to daydream about healing while the nurse was talking to him.

T.J finds himself standing in a long line. The people in line were conversing about their life – sharing their stories with one another explaining why they are there. Some stated, I have tried to love this man and he did not love me back, I am heart broken, I never felt love before – my family never loved me, my friends never loved me…One woman asked, Is this the place for Broken Hearts? Another woman uttered, Yes! this is the place to regain your self confidence, your self worth, and find love again. To experience this you must wait in the long lines and go through the emergency room entrance. The emergency room is in a dome shaped building with glass doors. People were so happy to be in the lines because they were looking to find love again, gain self confidence, live again,

respect others .... Live, Love and Experience...
that is what the City of Love gives.

T.J had one of the biggest audiences in the history
of the Big City of Love because he had hurt so
many people.

T.J was arrogant and cocky. T.J was a narcissist.
This was his personality, and people that are this
way do not realize they are, they consider this
normal behavior.

They don't realize it until they have inflicted a
great deal of pain on others or until they lose it
all. T.J wanted to be a better person. He just
didn't know how to accomplish this, and his life
continued a downward spiral until one day, it was
all gone; he had lost everything.

T.J deeply wanted to change, he wanted things to
be different. He even asked his friend at work,
where he can to find different type of woman; a
genuine woman who was not going to hurt him
and certainly not like the one who burned down
my mansion and caught him on fire.

T.J genuinely wanted to change, he wanted things
to be different. But all his attempts were
unsuccessful... Now he stands before the judge
with fear and trepidation in his heart awaiting his
sentence. His fate was sealed before he entered

the court because he was not able to change. He knew the judge was going to give him a harsh sentence.

Sometime after this, is when T.J started the relationship with Janice, the nurse; however, he still did not know what he wanted in life.

He conceals his feelings for Janice, as he is afraid to open his heart just to be hurt again. Although, he keeps his feelings to himself, he keeps her close because he knows that there is no way that he's going to ever find another woman as beautiful inside and out as this woman.

T.J finds himself in a unique predicament. A beautiful intelligent woman who likes him for who he is with his scars and imperfections. He is quite perplexed, but there is no denying the strong feelings that he has for Janice.

He's become a broken-down man and he doesn't know what to make of all this. Janice wants to be right by his side, flaws and all.

She has such an incredible love. A love that many dreams of, not like anything that one would envision in this lifetime. She has such a discerning spirit and soul and can look deep within to see the good in me; she sees my potential and is willing to take a chance with me

– she wants to love me whole heartedly – she just wants ME! So now T.J just feels empty inside because even though the nurse expressed her love for him, he is hesitant about sharing his feelings for her.

So, everything is cloudy in T.J's brain. The air feels stuffy and T.J is not sure what his next move should be. T.J leaves the therapy area, and he goes back to his room and he just went to bed, fell asleep and he had a dream.

T.J and Can-du are walking and talking along the beach. T.J is wearing all white, shirt sleeves rolled up, no shoes. It's an amazing day out. The sea is an intriguing turquoise blue and is so clear that you can see all the sea creatures swirl around. The sand is white as snow. The sun is bright. The clouds are pure white.

T.J is having the time of his life. It's hard to believe that this is the same man that wanted to commit suicide and turn to drugs. The same person that wanted to give up on the person that created him.

T.J never wanted to admit that he did believe in his creator. He did believe God himself brought him here to see himself as he is, as he could be, as he should be.

Can-du looks as all of a sudden T.J falls to his knees. His head is down, and tears start to run down his face uncontrollably. He couldn't stop the tears, and wipes his face and he looks up and says, Can-Du who are you?

Can-Du turns to him, and says I cannot lie. Even though I am the Concierge of the Big City of Love, I am also the angel of love. T.J raises his head and wipes his face, so Can-Du do you mean an angel from heaven, I mean like the Bible? Can-Du stands tall, opens his wings, and said, Yes, I'm the Angel of love from the Heavens and I am here to restore love to the world! There are many under-cover angels and we all have a mission to complete! Can-Du says T.J I serve a forgiving God. The Big City of Love is a place of forgiveness, and healing for the broken heart.

Can-Du says to T.J, it is no accident that you're here. But, in order for healing to begin, self-reflection must begin, forgiveness must begin! TJ it doesn't matter what you have been through please remember this, you are one of God's greatest creations!

T.J still had so many questions that needed to be answered. T.J looks to Can-Du, how long can I stay here, what happens when I leave?

Could I ever just visit the Big City of Love? Can-Du answers T.J, he says there are only three ways to get to the Big City of Love. First, by dreaming Secondly by fantasizing Lastly you are summoned by the Courts of Love.

Those are the only three ways that you can get to the Big City of Love. So, if you were to ever leave The Big City, it will be up to you, what happens to you.

We have given you the tools, the confidence, and we have restored your heart. You are greater today than you have ever been. Your life is now in your control. And you are forever welcome to The Big City of Love!

So, T.J walked along the beach a little more, and took a trail to the street that led to his hotel. He was staying in The Big City of Love. He took the elevator up to the hundredth floor into his penthouse suite. He opened the blinds wide with both hands and just stood there confident, that everything will work out!

Such an amazing view from all the way up here, T.J said, viewing the entire Big City of Love from his penthouse suite. The walls were completely glass and at this time the sun was going down, so you can see all the street lights, and all the cars in the streets of The Big City of Love.

People were out there, happy and enjoying themselves. And when T.J turned around Janice was standing right there. He had forgotten to lock the door.

He stood still for minute. He took both her hands. He looked straight in her eyes, she looked in his. He got on one knee and said I don't ever want to live without you will you please be my wife. And Janice looks deeply in his eyes and says, yes, I will and they embraced each other. T.J thought to himself, I know the only one that could have made this possible is Can-Du, and he mumbled silently from his mouth, thank you, Thank you! Thank you!

APPENDIX

Self-reflection -Yes, it's about that time to look in that mirror!

It's about that time to reach for your energy source and have a true understanding of your own personal current life values and motivations.

We are not perfect so there will come a time to come back and look in that mirror!

Self-Reflection time is the time to be honest about what we need to improve it could our own personality, fitness or even mindset.

Change the way you think to change the way you feel create your own atmosphere.

It's about that time to stop being judgmental but instead, let's start judging ourselves! let's start holding ourselves accountable for our own actions!

How can we seek greatness if we are not willing to create greatness within ourselves?

How can we seek a loving person if we don't truly love ourselves first how can we seek motivation when we ourselves are not even motivated?

How do we seek the real deal when indeed we are not even the real deal and even sometimes falsified, some of us speak a good game but truly do not know how to play the game and sometimes it is what it is just a game?

When will we set the standards of true realness without prejudice?

What happened to the standards of real love the standards of consistency?

On my journey of self-reflection, I reflect I analyze I start repairing all inaccuracies all inconsistency's and any misunderstandings that I may have presented I take all responsibility for all actions I can acknowledge my own wrong-doings and I correct them.

My greatest path to my motivation would be the door to my own self-reflection I live to be great therefore there is no other way then to I create my own greatness!!